Noiselessly, with[...]
undergrowth, a [...]
suddenly appeared[...]
materialized from t[...] ...e ground.

It was a vaguely humanoid figure, with two legs and two arms and so on. But it was at least twice Jonmac's height, its long limbs and body covered in short dark fur, all incredibly, inhumanly thin. Its round head was also furred, with no visible ears, a flat nose and a small thin mouth beneath eyes that were huge, round and dark. It was wrapped from neck to knees in many folds and swathes of delicate greyish cloth. And in one spidery hand it held a straight stick like a spear, with what looked like a sharpened splinter jutting from one end . . .

Douglas Hill
WORLD OF THE STIKS

BANTAM BOOKS

LONDON · NEW YORK · TORONTO · SYDNEY · AUCKLAND

WORLD OF THE STIKS

A BANTAM BOOK : 0 553 406558

First publication in Great Britain

PRINTING HISTORY
Bantam edition published 1994

Set in Linotype Palatino 11/12pt by
Hewer Text Composition Services, Edinburgh

Bantam Books are published by Transworld Publishers Ltd,
61–63 Uxbridge Road, Ealing, London W5 5SA,
in Australia by Transworld Publishers (Australia) Pty Ltd,
15–25 Helles Avenue, Moorebank, NSW 2170,
and in New Zealand by Transworld Publishers (NZ) Ltd,
3 William Pickering Drive, Albany, Auckland.

Made and printed in Great Britain by
Cox & Wyman Ltd, Reading, Berks.

PART ONE

INTRUDERS

1

A rattle of branches in a thicket brought Jonmac to a halt, hunched with tension.

In that forest, he knew, the spindly branches would rustle and tremble with the slightest breeze. But the day had been humid and overcast since morning, without the smallest hint of movement in the moist air.

Yet something had rattled the branches.

He stood still, listening hard, scanning the tangle of the forest all around him. But he heard nothing except the inner drum-beat of his own heart, and saw nothing except trees and brush and low undergrowth, shadowy in the grey light from the overcast sky.

The rattle from the thicket sounded again, and Jonmac jumped, making a rustle of his own among the low plants around his feet. Carefully he reached for a small, narrow plastic case on his belt, unclipping it, his hands damp with sweat.

It can't be anything, he told himself silently. There aren't supposed to be any dangerous life-forms on this planet.

Even so, his fingers tightened around the narrow plastic case. You never know, he reminded himself. That was practically the motto of human travellers to other planets. Including those who worked and space-travelled for the organization called EXTRA. They were all aware that no matter how thoroughly a planet had been studied, it

9

was still an *alien* world. And on such worlds – you never know.

Which is why Jonmac and all the EXTRA team on that planet carried the small plastic cases, called *vibes*. Their sonic vibrations did briefly painful but harmless things to the nerve-ends of any would-be attacker. As long as the attacker *had* nerve-ends.

At the same time, Jonmac was also remembering that he was quite a long way away from the EXTRA base. And he shouldn't have been. None of the team was supposed to go any distance into the forest alone, even with a vibe. Especially not Jonmac, who was not quite fourteen.

The silence around him continued, as thick and heavy as the humid air. Perhaps it's gone, Jonmac thought, whatever it was. Perhaps it was nothing at all. Slowly he began to take a silent step backwards, away from the dark thicket with its scary rattles. But his boot snagged on a twig jutting from one of the prickly plants that grew close to the ground, as thick as ferns. The twig snapped, echoingly loud in the stillness.

The noise was followed by something like an explosion within the thicket. As Jonmac swung up his weapon with a gasp, the scrawny branches clattered and something burst out of the thicket's depths.

Something about as long as Jonmac's arm and not much thicker, with a great many gauzy wings that fluttered wildly as it blundered with frantic haste into another small stand of trees.

Jonmac's gasp turned into a deep, relieved breath, and then a small laugh. Nothing to be afraid of, he told himself. Just another bug.

As harmless as everything we've found on this world.

Everything so far . . .

Clipping the vibe back on to his belt, he peered around for a moment, trying to decide what to do next. He was a thin, lanky boy, taller than the average for his age, wearing the plain grey tunic and trousers with sturdy boots that was standard garb for the EXTRA team. His face was fairly ordinary, with dark hair clipped short, strong cheekbones and heavy eyebrows. And his dark eyes usually held a look of expectant curiosity about what life would present to him next.

But just then, in the midst of that alien forest, he was looking and feeling dissatisfied. He had once again run into the old familiar clash between what he *wanted* to do and what he was *supposed* to do. Except in this case, for once, the choice wasn't all that obvious.

What he wanted to do was keep wandering around in the forest, hoping to find something interesting, enjoying the small excitement of being a lone explorer. What he was supposed to do was go back to the EXTRA base, sit down at his computer terminal and get on with school.

It should have been no contest – the exciting alien forest or boring old school. But in fact the forest hadn't been all that exciting, or even interesting, since he had wandered out into it during his midday break. Even the moment's fright from the noisy winged creature hadn't been anything new. He might have met the same thing two steps from the edge of the base.

On the other hand, school wasn't always boring, even when the teacher was an impersonal

11

microchip. That week's programme was history, and it had been dealing with that stormy time called the Disunion Decades, when so many of the old nations of Earth had torn themselves apart as savagely as possible. There was nothing boring about those violent, gory stories, even when told by a microchip.

Also, he reminded himself, there were people back at the base – such as the tough-minded leader of the team, not to mention Jonmac's own mother – who would have a few strong words to say to him if he went too far and stayed away too long. He might even be barred from leaving the base again, or from using the vid-library, or something.

I'd better go back, he told himself with a sigh. Then it occurred to him that he didn't have to go *straight* back the way he had come. Swing back in a half-circle, he thought. In case there *is* something interesting out here after all.

At least there was no danger of his getting lost. In his pocket he had a small responder, about the size of a pen, that would guide him back to the base with a directional signal – or guide others to him if he got into trouble and hit the panic button. So he set off with some confidence.

Even so, he tried to move quietly through the undergrowth, while peering into the shadows under every bush, into the blankness of every rivulet or pool. He did so as much out of curiosity as caution, for while the alien forest might not always have been wildly exciting, it was usually, to human eyes, interesting and strange.

Much of its strangeness came from the fact that its dense tangles were made by a profusion of twisted, entwined, skinny branches – and *only* branches. It was a forest of trees and plants that bore no leaves. Just scaly bark and plenty of thorns, all mostly a colourless dark grey, usually gleaming slightly in the prevailing dampness of the climate.

Some of the trees and shrubs were tall and spindly, with their thin branches reaching almost straight up, while others were more bushy with crooked branches spreading out in an interwoven riot. Even the small plants of the low ground cover were without leaves, making up for it with sharp twigs and prickles.

The trees and bushes tended to form large thickets and clusters, often incredibly snarled. But between the thickets the forest could still be fairly dense, with smaller clumps of trees or shrubs, and always the knee-high mesh of the ground cover. Still, in the thickets or out of them, every single plant in the forest had one thing in common, to a human eye.

Every one, with its absence of leaves and its peeling, flaky bark, looked naked and withered and utterly dead.

Yet in fact the trees and bushes were alive and healthy. They had large root systems reaching deep into the wet, dark soil, while odd white patches on the flaky bark took life-support somehow from the humid air. But even so it could be quite eerie and spooky in the depths of the forest, with the dim light making shadows among the seemingly lifeless trees, whose branches rattled like old bones and reached out like skeletal claws.

But the eeriness was part of the fun for Jonmac. It lent a bit of extra atmosphere to his wanderings.

And it made him try to be all the more alert as he followed his curving route back to the base. It was easier to be alert on such a silent day, when for once the forest was not filled with the rustling and rattling of bare branches stirred by a wind.

So he was able to hear quite clearly, over some distance, a sound that was both very familiar and very startling.

Human laughter.

The sound stopped Jonmac in his tracks. Ducking behind a nearby bush, he tried to peer through the branches towards the source of the sound, guiltily wondering if someone from the EXTRA base had come out looking for him. He crept forward, towards the place where the laughter had sounded, knowing he would be in trouble if he was found so far from the base. Then he stopped again, hearing another burst of laughter – followed by some words, not quite clear, in a sharp and ugly voice.

A voice that Jonmac had never heard before.

But it *had* to be someone he knew, he thought. There weren't any humans on the planet other than the EXTRA team. Were there?

He moved forward again, with agonizing care, feeling nervous sweat prickle on his skin as twigs and branches scraped rustlingly past him. Within a few moments he was able to peer through a skein of branches and see who was doing the laughing and talking. And he went entirely still, eyes wide with shock.

He was looking at a group of six men, standing or squatting in a narrow open area beside a broad, dark pool of water. The men seemed to be lounging in a casual sort of way, looking wholly at ease in the alien forest. All six were strangers to Jonmac.

And they clearly were not from EXTRA. Instead of the neat grey clothing, their garb was wildly colourful and crazily mismatched – an amazing variety of coats or jackets or tunics, trousers or leggings or overalls, colours ranging from lurid yellow to overripe purple.

In every case, too, their clothing was frayed and worn, stained and soiled. And the men themselves seemed as scruffy as their clothes. Many of them wore heavy beards, which Jonmac had almost never seen before on men's faces. And the sour smell of all six men reached out to his nostrils even without the benefit of a breeze.

While he took in all those details, Jonmac's main attention was caught by the weapons that the six men carried. Heavy, bulging, clumsy-looking things with short wide barrels, like a swollen mockery of a rifle, slung over the men's shoulders on thick straps. *Flamers*, Jonmac said to himself, recognizing the weapons from his vid-viewing. Frighteningly powerful, hugely expensive. Carried mostly by real professionals – on either side of the law.

Jonmac thought he could guess which side of the law the six unsightly strangers were on. But he was still well hidden and felt in no danger, so he continued to watch the men, half-wishing that he could see one of the flamers being fired. The wish had barely formed in his mind when it was granted.

A squat, thick-necked man with a heavy moustache, wearing a short blue cloak over a shirt and leggings that might once have been white, seemed particularly interested in the top of the nearest thicket. As Jonmac watched, the man suddenly grunted and without warning swung up his flamer and fired.

A blast of pure heat-energy, white-hot as a mini-bolt of lightning, lanced up with a sizzling hiss into the branches of a skinny tree. It struck a long, many-winged creature like the one that had startled Jonmac earlier. The creature vanished in a burst of smoke, instantly incinerated.

The man who had fired laughed another of the ugly, raucous laughs that Jonmac had heard before. 'That's me three bugs up,' he announced.

'Up on who?' one of the others snarled. 'Nobody's gamin' here 'cept you.'

One of the squatting men stood up, flamer dangling idly from one hand. He was tall and bulky with a tangled black beard, wearing a scarlet garment like a stained and ragged frock-coat.

'Leave it, Wace,' he told the squat moustached man, in a bass voice that seemed to rumble up from his sizeable belly. 'We don't need you settin' fire to the bush, shootin' bugs.'

'If anythin' could burn, all this wet,' muttered another man.

The moustached man, Wace, laughed again. 'Might hurry the Stiks right along, bit of fire.'

'Stiks'll be here,' said the deep-voiced man in the scarlet coat. 'They know where we are.'

Another man snickered unpleasantly. 'They need dustin', they'll be along.'

In his hiding-place, Jonmac was growing more and more uneasy. He knew who the men were talking about, and he thought he also knew *what* they were talking about. If he was right – if they meant what he thought by 'dusting' – some very bad trouble had arrived in that alien forest.

Then he twitched with new shock. Noiselessly, without any visible movement in the undergrowth, a weird and frightening figure had suddenly appeared near the six men, as if it had materialized from the air or risen from the ground.

It was a vaguely humanoid figure, with two legs and two arms and so on. But it was at least twice Jonmac's height, its long limbs and body covered in short dark fur, all incredibly, inhumanly thin. Its round head was also furred, with no visible ears, a flat nose and a small thin mouth beneath eyes that were huge, round and dark. It was wrapped from neck to knees in many folds and swathes of delicate greyish cloth. And in one spidery hand it held a straight stick like a spear, with what looked like a sharpened splinter jutting from one end.

The moustached man named Wace saw it first. With a muffled curse he whirled, bringing his flamer up to point it at the weird being.

2

But the man lowered the flamer at once, snarling something about sneaking Stiks coming out of nowhere. The tall, spindly being had not moved, its huge eyes unreadable as it silently stared at the six men. Then, behind it, with the same eerily noiseless suddenness, others like it began to emerge from the forest.

Altogether there were seven of them, looking more or less alike to a casual onlooker. But Jonmac was used to such beings by then, and had learned to see the differences. Some were taller than others, some had lighter-coloured fur, all had slight variations in the shape of their faces and features. They also differed slightly in how they draped and folded the cloth of their simple garments. And some held objects like crude axes instead of spears.

Most of them were also carrying large shapeless bundles, more of the dull grey cloth that their garments were made from. As they set some of them down, still in total silence, the humans produced large waterproof pouches that had lain hidden in the low undergrowth. The big man in the scarlet coat spoke a word or two, his bass voice too quiet for Jonmac to hear properly. And one of the tall thin beings replied, in a voice that rustled and crackled almost like a breeze through the brush.

The men drew small plastic cylinders from the pouches, handed them to the tall beings, then began gathering up the bundles of cloth. There was a brief flurry of talk among the men, and the scarlet-coated man growled something at the strange beings. That produced a few more bundles of the cloth from the beings, which seemed to satisfy the men.

By then Jonmac was feeling slightly sick. He didn't need to hear what was being said to know what was going on. He knew that he had been watching a process of *trade*. And he also knew, beyond doubt – remembering things he had viewed, and bits of EXTRA gossip – who and what the six men were. And what it was that they had just exchanged for the cloth.

It was confirmed for him at once. The strange beings were quickly but carefully opening the cylinders, pouring out some of the contents into their narrow, three-fingered hands. It seemed to be a fine, bluish powder, just as Jonmac expected. Some of the beings licked it up with their short black tongues, while others brought it to their flat noses and sniffed strongly to inhale the powder.

The six men watched with knowing grins. And the grins turned into unpleasant laughter as the powder instantly took effect. The tall beings began to sway and lurch, making faint noises like a very quiet howling. Slowly they stumbled away into the bush, their unsteady movements making far more noise than before, with the harsh laughter of the humans following them.

'Wish dust was that much fun fer me,' one of the men said as they gathered up their pouches and the cloth.

'We get home, we can buy any fun we want, much as we want,' another man said.

That led to some noisy, laughing discussion of the best sorts of fun to buy. Under cover of the noise, Jonmac slipped back through the brush, and got away unseen.

A glance at his responder confirmed his direction, and he set off at a run, as much as the thickets allowed. On the way, his mind replayed the images of what he had just seen, while shock and anger swelled within him.

He had seen a trade that should not have happened, by traders who should not have been there.

Also, and far worse, he had seen a vicious kind of cruelty that was truly criminal.

So he hurried back to the EXTRA base to report on what he had seen. And as he went, he thought about the legally permitted sorts of trading that were carried out by organizations like EXTRA, and the rules and codes of practice that had bound them from their very beginnings.

Long before those beginnings, the war-torn Disunion Decades – which Jonmac was learning about in history – had finally stuttered to an end, leaving what was left of humanity in a period of exhaustion and stagnation. But because the human spirit is hard to quell, it was not long before parts of the world began to climb out of those doldrums. Steadily, humanity's home planet was rebuilt and reborn into a time of healing and harmony, which became also an age of expansion and discovery.

That was because humans had, at last, found the means of flinging spaceships out across the unimaginable distances among the stars. Which led governments and big businesses to rush to take part in all the new extraterrestrial chances for progress and profit.

The first organization formed in that rush, which became the biggest, was EXTRA. It took its name from EXTRAterrestrial, but also from the first letters of EXploration and TRAde. As it grew, its starships scoured the galaxy for Earth-type planets where humans might live without costly life-support.

On such planets that lacked intelligent life, resources would be gathered or mined, colonies set up. So EXTRA grew richer and bigger. But on planets that did have life-forms with whom humans could communicate, EXTRA turned to trade. Whatever the aliens wanted, for whatever they had to offer.

Of course, it didn't always work. Some aliens could not grasp the concept of commerce. Some wanted too much for too little. Some were too advanced, too hostile or too indifferent to want anything from humans. But often enough, EXTRA's traders brought back large quantities of amazing things. And EXTRA grew richer still.

Yet its work was carefully regulated. Every trader in every team was also a highly-trained expert in one of the sciences, making full studies of the alien worlds and all their life-forms. The knowledge they gathered proved often as valuable as the alien goods. But the gathering was done within a huge range of laws and rules.

Every EXTRA worker had to learn what could be offered in trade and what could not. How first to approach an alien race, how to learn its ways without causing fear or shock or hostility. How to study an alien environment while causing the minimum of damage. How, above all, to survive.

While learning to avoid any breaches of alien customs and taboos, an EXTRA team was especially trained in the avoidance of violence. They had only protective technology, aside from the little 'vibes' – which were mostly harmless as weapons, and in any case were used only as a last resort.

Naturally, the history of EXTRA was full of tales of things that had gone wrong despite all the rules and good intentions. After all, alien planets were full of things that could not be foreseen because they had never even been dreamed of. It took a long time and an immense amount of work even to *begin* to understand an alien world and its inhabitants.

And when a team might think it was starting to understand, it was wise not to forget the space-traveller's basic motto. The one that said – *you never know*.

Jonmac had seen the motto's truth yet again, that day. There had always been other sorts of traders in space, on the fringes of the big organizations. Some of the other sort were just small freelance independents. But many of them were criminals. And those traders cared nothing for laws and regulations, cared nothing for the customs and beliefs of alien beings, cared nothing about scientific knowledge.

Those other traders went on to worlds where some group like EXTRA had already made contact with the aliens. There they traded as cheaply and quickly, and often brutally, as they needed. Then they got out, after making a quick killing – sometimes literally. Usually they left the careful links and communications between humans and

22

aliens, set up with huge care and effort, in ruins.

And now one of the worst of such illicit groups – one of the most notorious and ruthless – was *there*, in that alien forest where Jonmac was running. On the world of the Stiks.

That world was the second planet of a star named Bregele. The planet, known as Bregele II, had been found suitable for human life, with gravity and atmosphere much like Earth's. And, in the moist humid valleys where the climate hardly altered through the year, the planet proved to be full of life of its own.

The valleys were overgrown with dense forest, all as spindly and tangled and skeletal as the forest where Jonmac was running. And the forests supported a startling variety of creatures. Some were as small as pinheads, some as large as the flying thing that had scared Jonmac earlier. They had many legs or many wings or both, looking to humans more like giant insects than animals. Other creatures – some like huge leathery worms, some like spiny fish – lived in the pools and waterways of the forests.

And all of them, on land or in water, were peaceful, harmless vegetarians, feeding on the plant-life. Which helped to make the planet very attractive to the first explorers from EXTRA.

It became even more attractive when EXTRA met the humanoid aliens.

Properly, the aliens of that world were known as Bregelians. But humans often gave nicknames – not always kind or complimentary – to the beings they met on other worlds. Perhaps the skinny arms and legs of the aliens did look a bit like the scrawny bare branches of their trees. Certainly the aliens called themselves, in their rustling, crackling language, *Stikessi*.

Humans, inevitably, came to call them Stiks.

The Stiks were at a primitive level of development. Their clothing – the wrappings of cloth – was simple and minimal. Their spear-heads were extra-large thorns that grew on one sort of tree, and their axe-heads were segments of iron-hard bark from another tree. Besides clothes and weapons, they wore a few plain ornaments and made small crude carvings from polished wood. Otherwise, they seemed to own nothing.

They lived as nomads, drifting in small groups through their forest, unencumbered. They bent and wove branches into crude shelters each night. They gathered their food from the forest's produce, including hunting some of the larger creatures. They had no knowledge of fire, and no real need of it in their temperate forest.

Yet they were highly intelligent, quickly able to accept the idea of space-travelling humans who wanted to trade. As Jonmac's EXTRA team came to know the aliens better, they found them to be serene, tolerant and dignified, rarely showing aggression, often showing a lively sense of humour. And, surprisingly, they were not very curious at all about space travel or other worlds beyond their own.

They were also surprising in what they accepted as trade goods. They would take small cheap objects made of metal or glass, materials that were unknown on their world. But mostly the Stiks liked human *food*. They accepted most cereals, lentils and pulses, but they particularly liked the thick, gummy wafers of concentrated protein that were basic or emergency rations for space travellers. Jonmac found the stuff flavourless and dull, but the Stiks loved it.

In exchange, the aliens offered one of their world's most unusual resources – the cloth they wove.

The original fibre was produced by small insects that swarmed in the bush. Hand-woven by the Stiks' delicate fingers, the threads became a cloth of incredible toughness, virtually waterproof, yet as light and delicate as chiffon. The Stik word for it was *t'kii*, and the humans called it *ki*-cloth. It was highly prized on Earth, and highly profitable for EXTRA.

But now such rich pickings had brought the predators. Who seemed, in the brief glimpse that Jonmac had of them, to be ruthless, brutal, carelessly cruel – and very well-armed.

Jonmac had no idea at all what the EXTRA team could possibly do about them.

As the base came into his view through the surrounding brush, Jonmac hurtled through a small clump of trees and almost collided with his mother.

'Where have you *been*?' she demanded, her voice mingling anger and relief.

Jonmac looked at her, gathering his tumbling thoughts and dire news. She was a slender, small-boned woman, fair-haired, with large blue eyes in a sweetly pretty face. Yet for all her delicate looks, she had more than her share of the intelligence, courage and resilience needed to cope with life on other worlds.

Her name was Su Lowde, and she was an expert at the task of unravelling the inhuman tangle of alien languages. It was like breaking impossibly complex codes to which no one had the key. But Su was good at it, which made her a much valued employee of EXTRA.

When her husband, Jonmac's father, had gone his own way some twelve years earlier, Su had refused to leave her son behind on Earth, like an orphan, when she went to work on alien worlds. From then on Jonmac had gone with her everywhere. At almost fourteen, he was now an EXTRA apprentice, dreaming of fame and fortune when he became an adult trader.

'Well?' his mother said sharply. 'You were supposed to be at your schoolwork, and then I couldn't find you anywhere. You really must . . .'

'Su, listen!' Jonmac interrupted urgently. He had never called his mother anything except her name. 'I went into the bush, during break, and . . . and I saw . . .' He gulped, pausing, and she began to look worried as she finally noticed how upset he was. 'There were *men* out there! Trading with the Stiks! And . . . I think they're *Dusters*!'

Su went white. 'Dusters? How would you know, Jonnie?'

'I've seen them on vid-tapes,' he said impatiently. 'Who else would give Stiks some kind of *powder* for ki-cloth?'

'You saw that?' she asked. At his nod she grew even paler. 'They didn't see *you*?'

He shook his head. 'I was well hidden. Not even the Stiks knew I was there.'

'I hope not,' she said, gnawing her lip, glancing nervously around at the shadowed forest. 'Come on. We have to tell the others.'

'What do you think we can do?' Jonmac asked as they turned away towards the base.

'About the Dusters?' Su asked. 'I've no idea. But I hope we can do something. Before the Dusters destroy everything that we've got started on this planet.'

3

The base itself was built according to strict EXTRA requirements. A number of small buildings – portable pre-fabs made of plastishell – stood in a small clearing, placed so as to do the least possible damage to the forest. They were in a roughly triangular arrangement, with one point of the triangle occupied by the looming bulk of the cruiser-class starship that had brought them there.

Also by EXTRA rules, the ship had landed as lightly as possible, shutting off the stellarfield drive that carried it among the stars, descending on deflector-retros that did minimal harm to a planet's surface.

The ship rested on its angled undercarriage, looking to Jonmac as if it was raising its head to gaze longingly at the sky. Glancing at it as they entered the base, he wondered what kind of craft the Dusters used, and what *it* had done to the surface when it landed.

Most of the EXTRA team was out of sight, busy at their usual jobs. But one man came out of a building as Jonmac and Su walked towards it. He was a rangy man with a craggy face, pale blue eyes and tinges of grey showing in his cropped dark hair. Coln Robett, the leader of the team and starship pilot – a tough, experienced spaceman with a grimness about him that had at first made Jonmac nervous. Though he had noticed that the grimness was replaced by a

28

definite warmth whenever Robett was around Su Lowde.

That warmth was in his eyes then, along with a questioning look, when he saw Jonmac and his mother coming across the clearing.

'What's up?' he asked, his voice slightly hoarse as always. 'Was Jonmac playing truant?'

'He was out in the bush,' Su said tensely before Jonmac could speak. 'And he saw *Dusters*.'

Jonmac glared at her for not letting him tell his own news, then glared at Robett for raising his eyebrows in a sceptical way.

'They *were* Dusters!' he said firmly. 'Six of them, with flamers and everything. Handing out powder to the Stiks.'

'Where?' Robett asked.

Jonmac pointed. 'Over that way. About two kilometres . . .' His voice faltered when he remembered that that was four times farther from the base than he was supposed to go, alone.

But Robett merely raised his eyebrows again, without comment. 'Let's round up the others,' he said to Su.

It took only moments to bring the rest of the team from their work. They gathered in one of the buildings nearest the starship, in a room that was larger than most in those cramped pre-fabs, and that served as their communal eating-place or mess hall. The others – seven of them besides Jonmac, Su and Robett – were grumbling a little at having their work interrupted. But when Jonmac told them what he had seen, in vivid detail, the grumbling turned to nervous muttering.

One of the group also looked puzzled. He was a small, thin, long-nosed young man named Loysel, a techno-engineer who tended all the equipment and was also co-pilot of the starship. And he was a man of endless self-importance, which usually annoyed Jonmac.

'Just who are these people?' Loysel wanted to know. 'What do they think they're doing, trading here?'

'They're *Dusters*,' another man said, almost spitting the word as if it tasted foul. He was a stocky man with a bald head, named Pheng – Dr Pheng, for he was a medic as well as a space biologist. His tiny wife, Chani, was another medic and also an anthropologist, expert in alien cultures.

'That doesn't tell me who they are,' Loysel said tightly.

'There's been stuff about them on the vid,' Jonmac told him. 'Haven't you seen it?'

'I seldom watch the vid, I'm glad to say,' Loysel replied.

'Then let's review the data,' Robett said. 'The Dusters are a bunch of dangerous thugs who trade illicitly. Small groups of them move on to planets that have been opened up by EXTRA and others, and try to grab as much of the trade as they can by offering easy-dust to the aliens.'

'Ever heard of easy-dust?' Jonmac asked Loysel sarcastically.

The small man merely sniffed, without replying. Which was suitable, Jonmac thought, since that was what people mostly did with easy-dust. Sniff it.

On Earth, the dust was only a mild narcotic – cheap, easily produced, widely popular, legal in most countries. But it had proved to be dangerously addictive, or simply dangerous, to many of the humanoid aliens whose planets had been discovered by humans.

And the criminal traders called Dusters had used that fact to trap aliens into addiction on many worlds, in order to make their illicit trading quicker and more profitable.

'Filth, they are, trading that stuff,' snarled Dr Pheng, his face dark with anger. 'They swagger around, think they're glamorous, call themselves freebooters, privateers. But what they are is *filth* – polluting every place they go.'

'Dusters came to a planet called Xaster when we were there,' Chani Pheng explained. 'No one knew they were there, at first – not till the Xasterians started dying. They had an allergic reaction to the dust, stopped their breathing.'

Dr Pheng nodded bleakly. 'Luckily, that world was close enough to an EXTRA colony. They sent an armed force and got rid of those vermin.'

'No chance of that here,' Coln Robett said. 'A ship from the closest place would take months to reach us. Even any message we send will take weeks to get to EXTRA.'

'The Dusters could do a lot of damage in that time,' said a solidly built young woman with red hair. Her name was Parria, and she was an exo-psychologist, trained in the study of alien minds.

'Maybe we should get rid of 'em ourselves,' growled a tall, burly man whose name was Tranter, one of the two geologists on the team.

The shorter, compact man next to him, who was the other geologist, named Barranni, laughed harshly. 'Great idea. Our vibes against their flamers. Or do we just go and ask them nicely to leave?'

'There's only six of 'em,' Tranter muttered.

'We'll stay away from them,' Robett said flatly. 'Dusters don't worry much about the law even on civilized worlds. Here, with their firepower, they might wipe us out as soon as look at us.'

'So we do nothing?' asked a tall dark-skinned woman named Ndira, the team's astro-meteorologist. 'We just sit here while they stuff the Stiks with easy-dust?'

Robett gave her a wintry look. 'We have only two choices, aside from doing nothing at all. We pack up and leave the planet – or we try to convince the Stiks not to trade with them.'

'If we abandon the base and *leave*,' Loysel pointed out, 'EXTRA's licence to trade here would be instantly revoked. You *know* that.'

'We all know,' Su Lowde told him. 'That's the point. We really have only one choice – talking to the Stiks.'

'Do you know enough of their language to do that kind of talking?' Ndira asked.

'I can try,' Su said firmly.

Robett nodded. 'Try whatever you can,' he said to Su. 'You're the best hope we've got.'

'And the only one the Stiks've got,' said Dr Pheng darkly.

That brought the meeting to a rather gloomy end. Even so, no one seemed in a hurry to leave – except Loysel, who hurried off to the starship to send a message to EXTRA about the intruders. Jonmac listened briefly to Pheng telling Ndira some sickening tales of Duster activity on other worlds, then joined his mother and Coln Robett. They were talking with the psychologist, Parria, about the best way to warn the Stiks about the Dusters.

'We don't even know if their world has anything addictive on it,' Parria was saying doubtfully. 'How can you get the idea of addiction, and the danger, across to them?'

'They may already have the idea, Parria,' Su said bluntly. 'Many of them could already be hooked. We can work on that.'

'I hope you can,' Robett said. 'Because now we know why we've been getting fewer Stiks here to trade lately.'

The others nodded gloomily, including Jonmac. Despite all their scientific interests, they had been sent to the planet by EXTRA to *trade*. If the Dusters were pulling the Stiks away, taking most or all of the ki-cloth, the EXTRA team would be in trouble.

'All we can do,' Su pointed out, 'is what we're doing. Get on with our jobs, and hope we can make the Stiks see sense.'

Robett agreed, then turned away to speak to Loysel as the small man returned. And Su fixed her gaze on to her son.

'Back to work, then,' she said. 'Which means you too, Jonnie. No more roaming the bush. Glue yourself to that terminal.'

Jonmac grimaced. 'Can't I come with you? I could help . . .'

'No chance,' Su said with a smile. 'I know you've picked up bits of the Stik language, but that's *my* job. Your job is to do a fixed number of hours of school. Go to work, Jonnie.'

So Jonmac trudged unhappily off to a building on the far side of the base, where he and Su had their quarters. There, in his own tiny room, educational software awaited him. Though just then the history of the Disunion Decades seemed a lot less exciting than the real drama and danger that had arrived in their midst.

Over the next day or two, he was easily distracted. Watching computer-graphic images of ancient battles, he tended to see his own mental images of men in garish clothes shooting at innocent alien wildlife. Faced with data about historical invasions, he could think only of armed men bearing an addictive drug, invading the forests of peaceful alien beings.

When the sound of eerie voices rose, outside, he thought for a moment that they were in his imaginings. But then he realized with a start that they were truly there, and leaped to a window.

He saw a group of Stiks, carrying a few small bundles of ki-cloth, calling out softly as they walked on to the base. There were eleven in the group – one of the usual wandering groups that was like an extended family, with several males and females and children of various ages. It was not always easy to tell males from females among Stiks, though females often had lighter-coloured fur. While of course the children were smaller, and never carried weapons.

And one of the smaller, younger Stiks in that group, Jonmac was pleased to see, had unusually light fur, a warm yellowish colour that was almost golden.

Jonmac knew that one. In fact, he thought of that one as something of a friend.

The yellow-furred one was a young female whose family group visited the base quite often. From the start – because adult Stiks dealt with adult humans, and the other young ones in the group were very small and rather fearful – Jonmac had been mainly interested in the yellow-furred female. And she had returned his interest. Drawn to each other, they had somehow made contact, though wordless at first. But soon they had picked up scraps of each other's language, expanded with gestures, which were much used by Stiks normally. It had been slow and difficult and often frustrating, but little by little they had started talking.

He shut off his terminal and dashed outside. As the rest of the team emerged, some carrying the usual trade goods including packets of food, the young female moved away from her group to meet him.

'Rikil,' Jonmac said in greeting, trying to pronounce her name as she had first said it to him, knowing he probably wasn't getting it right.

'Onnak,' she replied in her soft crackly voice, unable like all Stiks to cope with js and ms.

For a moment they simply looked at each other, happily. Rikil was only a little shorter than him, but far thinner. Her large eyes looked even bigger within her narrow little face, her limbs looked almost frail, and her tiny three-fingered hands looked fragile as they toyed with the folds of her ki-cloth garment.

But to Jonmac, all that seemed totally normal. It seemed a long time since he had thought of Stiks as looking strange or weird. Gazing at Rikil's non-human features, Jonmac saw only the familiar face of a friend.

As always, their conversation had to move slowly. They spoke a mixture of their two languages, about simple things that they knew the words for, learning new words as they went. Yet they enjoyed it, and enjoyed each other's company. And Jonmac may not have realized just how much of the alien language he was picking up.

'Small . . . *t'kii*,' Jonmac said, making a gesture that indicated a small amount, pointing to the bundles of cloth brought by the Stiks.

Rikil jerked her head in a movement that meant 'yes'. 'Small,' she agreed. *'T'kii* goes . . . to *hikisti*.' She touched her tiny nose, sniffing sharply.

Jonmac blinked. He had never heard the word before, but the gesture said that it was the Stik word for the easy-dust.

'Stikessi . . . want *hikisti*?' he asked hesitantly.

A shadow seemed to pass across Rikil's enormous eyes. She held up one hand, as if holding out something for Jonmac to see. 'Stikessi want,' she said. She held up her other hand. 'Stikessi not want.' Then she closed her little fists and brought them together, knuckles rapping each other sharply, while she peered at Jonmac to see if he understood.

Slowly he nodded. She was saying that the Stiks were divided among themselves over the easy-dust. Arguing, or fighting, or colliding in some way, in favour or opposed.

He pointed to the rest of her group – who were listening impassively to Su Lowde as she said something slowly and carefully in the alien language. 'They like *hikisti*?' he asked. 'Rikil like?'

She made a sharp jerky movement that he knew was 'no'. 'Not like. Rikil not like.'

She paused, her small face wrinkling as she tried to work out how to say something. Finally she held up one hand again. 'Like *hikisti*,' she said, then opened the fingers of that hand and

36

made a sweeping circle in the air. At once her other hand came up. 'Not like,' she said – and those fingers pinched together and made only a tiny movement.

Jonmac understood, with a sinking heart. She was saying that many more Stiks were in favour of the dust than were opposed. Which is why not many have been coming here lately, he thought. And why this group have brought so little of the cloth.

'*Hikisti* . . . *bad*,' he told Rikil. To emphasise the point, he made sniffing movements, then clutched at his stomach and throat, rolling his eyes, grimacing and moaning. At first Rikil thought it was funny, and made the soft breathy humming that was Stik laughter. But then she stopped as she grasped his meaning.

'Bad,' she said, as if tasting the word, then jerked her head sharply in the gesture that meant yes.

At that moment they were distracted. Among the group of Stiks and humans, voices were being raised on both sides. That was something new, for Stiks were usually quiet-spoken, self-contained. Jonmac could hear his mother's voice, also raised, repeating some Stik phrases with insistence and anxiety in her voice. At the same time Coln Robett was saying something to Su, just as insistently, while several of the Stiks were also all talking at once.

In the hubbub Jonmac couldn't quite catch any of the words in either language. But he could see the Stiks repeating the sharp gesture that meant 'no'. He could also see, oddly, that the Stiks all seemed to be trembling. And the sounds of their words were being mangled because they had begun a rapid-fire stuttering.

Rikil watched with Jonmac, and an even darker shadow showed in her eyes. She took a step away, her own delicate limbs beginning to tremble.

'On-n-n-ak,' she said, as if in farewell, stuttering like the adults. Then she turned away to rejoin her group.

By then the loud exchange of words had ended. As Rikil rejoined them, the Stiks stalked silently away – ignoring a last few words from Su that sounded like an appeal.

At the edge of the clearing, Rikil looked back at Jonmac. Raising one hand, she touched the fingertips briefly to her brow, then stretched that hand out towards Jonmac, fingers fluttering.

An instant later, they had melted into the forest and were gone.

4

'They've *never* raised their voices before,' Su was saying unhappily as Jonmac pushed in among the others, clustered around her. 'And I've never seen them so distressed . . . the way they shook, and the stuttering . . .'

'Was that distress?' Coln Robett asked, frowning. 'I wondered if they were showing anger, or fear.'

Su waved a hand vaguely. 'All those things together, I suppose. Anyway, they got upset. We upset them. Which is exactly the *last* thing we wanted to do.'

'Who cares if a few primitives get upset?' Loysel asked with a sniff. 'We're here to trade with them, not mother them.'

'Oh, go play with some hardware, Loysel,' Su said tiredly. 'If we upset them, they'll be less keen on trading.'

'Not if they're still keen on our goods,' big Tranter said.

'But that's the problem,' Su told him. 'Most Stiks *aren't* keen any more. Most of them in this forest prefer to trade for easy-dust – because the addiction is spreading like a plague.' She sighed. 'That's what has really upset this group, today. They're some of the few Stiks trying to stay clear of the dust. They're afraid of it, and afraid of the Dusters, and not very happy with any humans at all. They really didn't like being lectured about the dangers of the dust, which they're well aware of.'

Loysel raised an eyebrow. 'Are you *sure* of all that? Do you really understand them that well?'

Su shrugged, looking so weary and unhappy that Jonmac wanted to hug her. 'I don't feel sure of too much, if you want the truth. But that's the gist of what they said, as far as I could tell.'

'They were speaking awfully fast,' Parria said sympathetically.

Su nodded. 'That made it harder. I'm still not even sure that I got the word they use for the dust. *Hikit* or something . . .'

'That should have been your first priority,' Loysel said with another sniff.

Jonmac scowled at him. 'The word is *hikisti*,' he said angrily.

'How do you know that, Jonnie?' Su asked. And then she smiled, realizing, before he could reply. 'Oh, of course – your little friend.'

Jonmac nodded. 'And she said . . .'

But Su had turned away, not listening. As if anything else that was said between Jonmac and his 'little friend' could be of no value. It was one of the most infuriating things an adult could do, Jonmac thought irately, and he had to clench his teeth to keep from saying so right then, very loudly.

'Anyway,' Su was saying, 'one thing I am sure of. As sure as anyone can be,' she added with a scowl at Loysel. 'The majority of Stiks in this forest are trading with the Dusters. And I think this group, today, wants us to do something. Not just lecture them about the dust. I think they feel that if we believe trading for dust is so bad, we should put a stop to it.'

'Good thinking,' Tranter muttered.

'Maybe they blame us,' Parria added, 'because

40

the dust was brought by other humans after we got here.'

'All the more reason for us to *do* somethin' about it,' Tranter growled.

Robett shook his head. 'There's still nothing we can do, as far as I can see.'

'Then is the trade finished?' Loysel asked. 'Are these Stiks today never coming back?'

'I don't honestly know,' Su replied. 'And I don't know if any others will come any more.'

'Let's not get too gloomy before we have to,' Robett said as they all looked worriedly at one another. 'Before long the other Stiks may find out what the dust can do to them, long-term, and might turn against it.'

'Or the Dusters might fall into a bog an' drown,' Tranter added.

Loysel pursed his lips. 'That's not the most promising set of possibilities.'

'Maybe not,' Robett told him, 'but they're all we've got. So we'll just wait and see.'

'That's it,' Barranni said with a humourless grin. 'Remember the principle, Loysie-boy. *You never know.*'

Still, it was clear that everyone was downcast and pessimistic about the future of their trade on the planet. And they grew more so as time went on. Trade dwindled almost to nothing. Fewer and fewer Stiks came to the base, and much less often, with much less ki-cloth.

The scientific work of the team went on during those days, but even that could lead to more gloom. As when the Phengs came back from one excursion into the forest, and Tranter and Barranni from another, with the same tale to

41

tell. They had spotted the Dusters carrying on a thriving trade, at different places in the bush.

'Giving out piddling bits of dust,' Barranni reported angrily, 'and taking in *bales* of cloth. Got to be costing them almost nothing. Must be making a fortune.'

'An' Stiks fulla dust, all over the place,' Tranter put in. 'Fallin' over, crawlin' around in the bush . . .'

'We saw just the same,' Chani Pheng agreed, sadness in her eyes. 'It is so terrible. The Stiks are being *ruined*!'

The rest of them murmured, sharing her distress and her pity for the addicted aliens.

'Looks like the Dusters stay on the move,' Coln Robett said. 'They've been spotted in different places in the bush each time. So they're going to the Stiks, not waiting for the Stiks to come to them.'

Barranni gave a sour laugh. 'Maybe they keep moving because they think Tranter might borrow a Stik spear and come after them.'

'Now there's an idea,' Tranter said, forcing a half-grin.

But no one else joined in the attempt at humour, and the conversation – like so many during those empty days and weeks – soon faded and died as everyone wandered off to deal with their gloom in their own way.

Jonmac was finding it all particularly hard to deal with, since he was on his own much of the time as the others tried to lose themselves in their other work. Also, Rikil and her family group had visited the base only once during all those weeks. And they had stayed so briefly that he and Rikil had only been able to exchange greetings. Yet as she left she had again made the odd gesture – a hand touching her brow, then extended, fluttering, towards Jonmac.

Since then, he had been waiting and longing for her to return. He missed her a great deal, missed the special quality of her presence. She had always been fascinating to Jonmac because of her non-human difference – but her company had become more enjoyable because they had been getting *past* their differences. Communicating more easily, extending their friendship.

He felt sure that she liked him in the same way. Just as he was fairly sure that her fluttering gesture was a Stik expression of friendship. At least, that's what he wanted it to be.

What he feared was that it was their way of saying goodbye. And that she might not come again, now that so much had changed in the forest.

He would have liked to talk about Rikil with his mother, but Su was as busy and preoccupied as everyone else, with little time for important talk with Jonmac. Of course, she and some of the others found time to talk *to* him, as adults always did. Giving orders, making comments and announcements, all that. But he wanted to talk *with* someone, preferably someone of his own age. On that world, that meant Rikil.

To be fair, his mother didn't usually ignore him. But in those weeks she was working long hours, with fierce concentration, trying to grasp as much of the Stik language as possible. The idea was that she would keep trying to talk to any and all Stiks about the dangers of the trade in easy-dust. Talk was the team's only real weapon, as Robett had said, and Su was trying to make it as effective as possible.

Jonmac had offered to help her – but she had said no, thanking him in a vague way like patting him on the head. Even though she had praised him for coming up with the Stik word for easy-dust. 'You've got a bit of a knack for language, Jonnie,' she had said.

Still, she had no real idea of how much of the Stik language he had picked up. Though in the end, he knew, it probably didn't matter. He probably couldn't help her because he had no *training* in the study of alien languages.

Nor, as Su often pointed out, would he ever get training in anything until he had gone through all the earlier stages of his schooling.

So he sat glumly for some part of every day at his terminal, being educated. And the rest of the time, just as glumly, he idled around the base, doing odd jobs and chores – finding that almost as boring as doing nothing, and all the time missing Rikil.

Until, at last, on impulse, he put an end to boredom. One day, when his schoolwork was done and everyone else was inside, hard at work, he slipped off into the forest. For something to do, to see what he could see. And with the vague hope that he and Rikil might somehow cross paths.

It was a foolish hope, as he well knew. In that vast forest he might wander for days without seeing any Stiks, let alone a particular one. So he was really planning just to enjoy the wandering and exploring. Though he also planned, if he met any Stiks at all, to try to ask them where he might find Rikil's family group.

After some while, a fine rain began to fall – a

44

typical rain in that forest, almost a mist of minute droplets drifting like cool steam. But his EXTRA uniform was water-resistant, and he enjoyed the rain's coolness since he had got warm and sweaty struggling through thick undergrowth up a long steady slope. At the top of the slope, starting down the other side, he tipped his face up to the rain.

In that moment a swarm of tiny black winged things swooped around his head. Swatting at them, not looking where he was going, he got a foot tangled in a knot of prickly brush and went sprawling.

He lay there for a moment, spitting out a bit of flaky twig, swiping angrily at one or two remaining winged things. Then, from his prone position, he noticed that he could see for what, in that forest, was quite a distance. Because he was looking through the lower trunks of the trees and bushes, rather than through the more dense and tangled branches.

At first, because of the poor light and the rain, he thought he was seeing a group of Stiks – standing in a clearing, a good many metres away. It looked like an unusual clearing, too, for it seemed to have no plant life in it. Just a broad expanse of bare black earth.

He started to get up, then paused and peered more intently. They aren't *moving*, he thought. Just standing there, perfectly still. With their eyes closed, as if asleep on their feet.

He crept slowly forward, trying to move quietly. Still the group of Stiks stayed motionless. Then, as he drew nearer and could see more clearly, he realized that they weren't really Stiks at all.

They looked like Stiks in most ways, but with

45

some important differences. Not only were they unmoving – they were also neither clothed nor covered with fur. They looked as if they had been *skinned* – perfectly bare, perfectly smooth, a shiny reddish-brown colour, glistening like polished wood.

Nervously, Jonmac stepped into the clearing, in among the still, glistening figures. And then he understood what they were, and why they did not move.

He was looking at statues.

5

For some time Jonmac wandered around the clearing, among the life-size figures, marvelling. During that time the misty rain stopped and some breaks in the clouds allowed pale sunlight to filter down into the forest. In that light the surface of the statues gleamed even more brightly. It was an amazing surface, Jonmac found – hard and silky smooth to the touch, polished and quite flawless.

But otherwise the statues were amazing likenesses of Stiks. Carved with uncanny artistry, showing every detailed curve and crease and line of the alien bodies. And each one was different, in size and shape and features, as individual Stiks were different.

Jonmac wondered if they actually did represent particular Stiks. Perhaps they were there to honour the dead, the ancestors, which he knew was a common practice among primitives. Perhaps they marked actual graves – though they would have to be very special graves, he thought.

He had counted thirty-two of the statues scattered around the clearing, each standing in plenty of space. Obviously the Stiks, even of that one area of the forest, would have had more dead than that over the generations. So either these thirty-two were very special, or there were other clearings with other statues . . .

But by then he was thinking less of what the

statues might *be*, as his mind filled with visions of what they might *become*.

They could become his personal path to fame and fortune.

Even an EXTRA apprentice like himself knew about the hunger, on Earth, among rich people and museums and the like, for art and artefacts from other worlds. Every space trader knew the stories of people who had brought back even small alien objects and had sold them for quite staggering sums. Such stories, in fact, were one of the things that drew people to join organizations like EXTRA, and to go into space.

And now Jonmac might have his own story told, with awe and envy, in space-going circles. If he and the team could get the Stiks to part with any of the statues, their fortunes were made. Just one or two of the statues might be worth as much as a whole shipload of ki-cloth. Not just because the statues were exotic and alien, but because in their own right, as works of art, they were beautiful.

We'll be rich, he thought, dazed by his visions. And I'll be the one who made the discovery. The space-trader who had his biggest coup before he was fourteen.

He thought of taking one of the smaller statues back to the base, right then, to show the others. But he was still an EXTRA trader, for all his youth, trained to be ultra-careful in dealings with aliens and their possessions. Leave them, he told himself. Until we know more about them.

One thing he wanted to know, for instance, was how the things stayed so firmly upright and balanced. They had no bases or anything, but just stood on their own narrow three-toed feet. Reaching out, he pushed lightly and experimentally at a statue's shoulder. It did not budge. Pushing harder, and harder still, he found that he could only make it sway a tiny amount. And it returned to its upright position at once when he stopped.

That settles that, he thought. I couldn't take one back if I wanted.

He peered down at the feet, wondering what it was that held the statue so firmly fixed. Maybe a bit sticks down underneath, he thought, and is driven into the ground. But it didn't matter. Things like that could be discovered later.

He turned quickly away, bursting with the need to tell everyone. Setting off at a half-trot, he began to rehearse the scene. He'd wait till they were all together, maybe in the mess hall. Then he'd be cool and casual at first, leading up to it until they were all mystified, before dropping his bombshell.

He grinned as he imagined the reactions. His mother would be proud; Coln and the others would be impressed. Even Loysel would have to choke back his sneering. And when the news got to EXTRA, on Earth, they'd probably give him full trader status right then, without making him grind through the rest of his apprenticeship.

They might even give my name to the statues, he thought dreamily. Especially if they were bought by a big art gallery or museum. They'd have a special display, with a big sign. Something like 'THE LOWDE DISCOVERY: the art of the Stikessi . . .'

At that moment his dream of glory vanished as he stepped into a shallow depression in the ground, half-filled with muddy water. He yelped, then said a rude word as he pulled his dripping foot from the puddle. Balancing on one foot, trying to shake some of the clammy wetness from the other, he nearly toppled over, which made him swear again.

Then he jerked and spun round with surprise, as behind him rose the whispery humming of Stik laughter.

Rikil stood there, her great eyes bright with amusement. And around her, having emerged soundlessly from the bush, were the other Stiks, large and small, of her family group.

They had clearly been gathering food. Some of them held objects like large nuts or small vegetables, while others carried the bodies of some of the larger bug-like wildlife, legs or wings drooping. But Jonmac was looking mainly at his friend.

'Rikil,' he greeted her.

'Onnak,' she replied, stepping towards him. 'Onnak long way . . . in forest,' she added.

Jonmac glanced around, realizing that he had again come a lot farther than he was supposed to. Carefully he sorted out the right Stik words. 'In forest . . . see . . . Rikil.'

She cocked her head on one side, then laughed softly with a quick gesture. '*Nik'littin*, Onnak.'

That meant 'welcome' or 'glad to see you', he knew, which was encouraging. He looked at the other Stiks, all seeming ready to stay there indefinitely while the young ones talked. But for Jonmac it was no time for small talk or language practice. The meeting with Rikil and that group was a heaven-sent opportunity.

Be cool now, he told himself. Get into it slowly and carefully.

'Stikessi trade?' he asked Rikil. That was one word that most Stiks definitely knew.

Rikil spread her delicate fingers, then indicated the others who also carried none of the alien cloth beyond their garments. 'No *t'kii*.'

Jonmac searched for the right words. 'Trade other? Different? Not *t'kii*?'

Rikil put her head on one side again, her bright eyes dimming a little as was the way with Stiks when they were troubled in any way. I'm just confusing her, Jonmac thought. Say it clearly.

He pointed in the direction of the clearing with the statues, no longer visible through the brush. 'There,' he said, combining Stik and human words. 'Things stand. Look like Stikessi.'

He saw Rikil's eyes grow even darker, as if she was even more confused. And the adult Stiks, murmuring to one another, began to move closer, watching Jonmac, their own eyes darkening.

'Look like?' Rikil repeated. Then she made the abrupt gesture that meant 'no', with a gasping intake of breath.

She hasn't got it, Jonmac thought. 'There,' he said again, pointing. 'Things like Stikessi.' He paused, thinking hard – and then somehow his mind produced exactly the combination of Stik words that he needed.

'In the place of bare earth,' he said, still pointing.

The eyes of every one of the Stiks went entirely black. Rikil gave her little gasp again, but the sound was lost as the adult Stiks began a volley of harsh, crackling speech. Several of them lunged towards Jonmac while Rikil spun to face them and cried out, words he didn't know.

He barely began to feel bewilderment and a first stab of fright, barely started a jerky backward step away from the suddenly looming, frightening aliens.

He saw a sudden flicker of movement on the edge of his vision. Before he could react, something slammed with a ferocious impact against the side of his head. Pain like white fire exploded through his skull, and he was flung limp and twitching and stunned to the ground.

Though not quite unconscious, he found that his arms and legs would not respond when he wanted them to move. Through the agony of his head he could hear the crackly voices of the Stiks, still sounding loud and furious. And though his vision was blurred and not fully focused, he was sure that the yellow-furred figure of Rikil was standing almost directly over him, thin legs straddling his body – as if she was protecting him, holding the others off.

The noise of the Stiks seemed to go on endlessly, with Rikil making quite a lot of it. Jonmac drifted in and out of consciousness a few times, so that he lost track of how long he lay there. When he finally came more fully awake, regaining some shaky control over his body, the noise of the Stiks had come to an end.

He sat up weakly, his head a ball of agony. He had been struck by a Stik axe, he knew, having seen it clearly even in that moment's glimpse. But he had the idea that somehow the axe had been *turned*, so only the flat side had struck him. Had Rikil tried to block the attacker's arm? And a coldness swept through him as he realized that he would no longer be alive if the axe's hardened edge had hit him.

Fearfully he looked around. But no Stiks remained

to threaten him. Just Rikil – standing alone several paces away, gazing at him with enormous darkened eyes.

'Rikil . . .' Jonmac gasped. But he had no idea what to say, or ask. And then he had to roll to one side, to be violently sick into the undergrowth.

At last, groaning, he turned to face her again. She had not moved, regarding him steadily.

'Onnak . . . g-go,' she said. Her voice quavered with a hint of the distressed stuttering he had heard before. And her frail body was trembling.

'Rikil,' he said shakily, groping for words. 'What . . . ? Why did they . . . ?'

She broke in with a burst of her own language, then slowed, going back to the awkward mixture of their two languages that they usually spoke. 'Onnak must not come . . . to place of bare earth. Not come. Not c-come.'

Her voice grew more agitated as she repeated the words, until she trailed off into another spate of Stik words that Jonmac couldn't follow. But the message was clear enough.

He had trespassed. He had crossed the line that EXTRA traders worried about as much as anything. He had violated a taboo, had intruded into some ultra-important Stik place.

Obviously the statues were greatly valued by the Stiks, probably sacred or something. And he had blundered along like a stupid kid and asked them to trade the objects of veneration.

He knew he was lucky to be alive. And he knew, remembering his blurred view of Rikil standing over him, that he was alive because she had saved him.

'I'm sorry, Rikil,' he said wretchedly, struggling to his feet. 'I didn't know. I meant no harm . . .'

But he was speaking in his own language, and she visibly didn't understand.

'On-n-ak m-must g-g-go,' she said, her voice faltering even more. 'Must n-not c-come to Stikessi. M-must n-not come to R-rikil. M-must n-not c-come to f-forest. Must *n-not*!'

Jonmac moved unsteadily towards her, reaching out, swaying as the shock of her words struck him. But she moved back and away, with delicate grace. And the brush silently swallowed her up.

'Rikil!' he cried. But no sound followed, except the rattle of branches in a small gusting breeze.

He stood where he was for a long, silent moment, sinking into misery and self-loathing that were more painful than his bleeding, throbbing head wound. He called Rikil's name, he yelled a wordless cry at the indifferent forest. He wanted to fall back on to the ground and curl up in a heap. He wanted to weep and writhe and scream and break things.

In the end, he simply turned around and set off, drooping and stumbling, for home.

He knew he would never forget Rikil's final words. It occurred to him that she might have told him to stay out of the forest partly because other Stiks might still try to kill him for his trespass. But it didn't matter. She had effectively told him to stay away – from her.

And she had not made the brow-touching, fluttering gesture that probably spelled friendship.

He felt the sting of unshed tears behind his eyes as he stumbled on. And shame and loss and wretchedness rose to fill him like a flood.

I've wrecked it, he thought despairingly. Not only Rikil and me but maybe the whole trade, everything. I've ruined it. I thought I was going to be so rich and successful – but now my career could be finished before it starts. And everything's ruined for everyone else, too.

He had no idea how he was going to face the team, how he would be able to face them. There would probably also be penalties from EXTRA for the damage he had done, breaking such a basic rule. But just then, he could imagine no greater punishment than his own bitter shame, and the reproach and disgrace he knew he would face when he told the others what he had done.

6

In the end, he wasn't able to tell them anything at all.

He found his way back to the base almost by instinct, barely able to focus on his responder as his vision grew blurry again. He was like a hurt animal yearning for its den, struggling on with his wound still bleeding. Becoming more unsteady on his feet, he fell once or twice without really knowing it – just as he didn't register the sharp twigs and thorns that stabbed at him in the thickets. Such small hurts could not touch him in the midst of his greater pain, the waves of misery sweeping through him.

When he reached the base, he was weaving and staggering, the last of his strength drained away. He heard a cry of horror in his mother's voice, but when strong hands lifted him from his feet he didn't see whose they were. Unconsciousness was rising to take him, and he fell with gladness into its pain-free dark.

When he awoke, he was in his own narrow bunk in his room with Su sitting beside him looking tense and worried. But her smile when he opened his eyes was like sunlight after rain.

'Jonnie.' She reached down to stroke his brow, staying carefully clear of the bandage on the side of his head. 'How do you feel?'

'All right, I suppose,' he mumbled. 'Kind of dizzy.'

'I'm not surprised,' Su said. 'You have a serious

concussion. Dr Pheng thought at first that your skull might be fractured. What was it, Jonnie? What happened?'

'I . . .' he began, then stopped. Her question brought it all back – every bit of the terrible, torturing mixture of feelings that had swept over him when Rikil sent him away. The misery rose in him like bile, choking him, silencing him. Looking at his mother, remembering Rikil, he could not bear the thought that Su might also despise him for what had happened.

'I fell,' he said lamely at last, not meeting Su's eyes. 'I . . . I was running in the bush, and I tripped and hit my head.'

Su nodded. 'I thought it was something like that. Pheng says it's amazing that you could find your way back. You really looked half-dead when you staggered in.' She stroked his brow again. 'You should have stayed where you were, and called for help.'

'I suppose,' he said dully. Of course he could have used his responder to bring them to him. But he hadn't been thinking properly through all that misery and pain. He doubted if he was thinking properly yet.

Several times, during the days that followed, he braced himself to tell his mother the truth of what he had done in the forest. Each time, he hesitated and drew back, unable to face her reaction or the reaction of the others. So he remained silent in his misery while Pheng tended his hurts and Su fussed over him and the others came to sympathize. And if any of them noticed that he seemed unusually quiet and withdrawn, in those days, they assumed it was an after-effect of the accident.

In any case, during that time, everyone on the base was feeling fairly withdrawn, and increasingly depressed. Because everything had stopped. Their trade had dried up completely.

Even the few Stiks who disliked the easy-dust had now, apparently, abandoned the trade with the team. And when members of the team ranged out through the forest, for various scientific purposes, they saw no signs of Stiks anywhere.

'If they're still around,' Barranni said one night, 'they're sure staying out of our way.'

Dr Pheng nodded. 'It feels as if they've put us in quarantine.'

'Right,' Barranni agreed. 'Like we're a no-go area for them.'

'I wonder if it's the Dusters,' Su said thoughtfully. 'If they've somehow managed to turn all the Stiks against us.'

Robett frowned. 'No way of knowing unless we can talk to some Stiks and ask them.'

'Oughta send Jonnie out,' Tranter said with a grin. 'To find that girlfriend of his an' ask *her*.'

Jonmac had been listening in silence, as he usually did in those dismal days. By then his head injury was almost fully healed, but his inner misery had not eased at all. If anything, it had grown worse as he watched the others grow despondent at the collapse of the trade. The terrible gnawing pain of guilt swelled within him as each day went by. Each further day when he had not told the truth, had not confessed that it was his fault.

Guilt and misery surged up within him again, then, at Tranter's mention of Rikil. He felt himself flush as he hunched his shoulders and stared at the floor, not meeting anyone's eye. But no one

58

was looking at him, because Loysel had joined the discussion, angrily.

'Who cares *why* the Stiks aren't coming?' the little man snapped. 'The point is that the trade has stopped. It's *over*. And I don't see the point of us just going on sitting around doing nothing.'

'We're not,' Chani said defensively. 'All our studies . . .'

Loysel ignored her. 'You all *know* what the EXTRA guidelines are. Every minute that we stay here, with the trade at an end, is a drain on the company's resources.'

'Always the company man,' Ndira murmured acidly.

'Why not?' Loysel demanded. 'I want to keep my job – don't you? And sitting here, expensively, with no cloth coming in, is not the way to do it. I say it's time to cut our losses and leave the planet.'

'That'd make the Dusters happy,' Barranni drawled.

'They're happy *now*,' Loysel said sharply. 'They're the only ones trading.'

'He has a point,' Parria said uneasily.

'So he has,' Robett said, glancing around at all of them. 'Most of us have probably had a thought or two, these last days, about pulling out. But . . .' He paused, as if unsure of his words. 'I just have a feeling. That we shouldn't be too quick to leave.'

'That *feeling* could be very expensive,' Loysel told him.

'It could,' Robett said. 'But the expense would be worth it if we found that this was just a temporary lapse, and that the Stiks would be back.'

As some of the others muttered their agreement, Loysel glared around. 'I still say we'd be foolish to take such a gamble.'

Robett shrugged. 'A gamble is only foolish if you don't win. And anyway, it won't affect your career, Loysel. You can blame it all on me.'

Loysel sniffed, looking as if he planned to do just that, while Parria still looked uneasy. But the rest of them were nodding their heads determinedly.

'We're agreed, Coln,' Su said. 'For myself, I'd really like to try to find out what's gone wrong.'

'Yeah,' Tranter said. 'An' I wouldn't wanta look like we'd been chased away by Dusters.'

Jonmac hunched deeper in his chair, feeling his misery wrapping around him like an almost visible cloud. For once he sided with Loysel, wishing that the team *would* pack up and leave the planet. Because then he could hope to leave his guilt and his shame behind. Then no one would ever need to know what he had done, and he and Su could go to some other job for EXTRA on some other planet, and forget all about the Stiks.

But instead they were going to stay. Which meant, he thought dismally, that any moment of any day might bring some new development that would expose his guilty secret.

In fact that development, that exposure, happened the very next morning.

Jonmac was at his terminal, gloomily trying to get on with his schoolwork, when he heard his mother's exclamation from another part of their quarters.

'Look at *this*!' she said. 'Walking in as if they own the place!'

For a terrible moment Jonmac was sure that some Stiks had come to the base, and guilt made him certain that they would be there to tell everyone what he had done. But when he glanced from his window he saw not Stiks, but something else that was nearly as alarming.

The six Dusters. Swaggering on to the base, flamers slung on their shoulders, looking around with grins or sneers.

As the EXTRA team came warily out to meet them, Su and Jonmac hurried out as well, joining the others in time to hear Coln Robett ask them what they wanted. Which made their leader – the big bearded man in the long scarlet coat – laugh unpleasantly.

'Come fer a visit, us,' he rumbled, and the other Dusters echoed his laughter. 'Friendly visit, to see how things're goin' here. How business is.'

'That's not your concern,' Robett said flatly.

The Duster leader grinned. 'No need to be like that. Just showin' a friendly interest.' He glanced at the other EXTRA people. 'Name's Strake, me – sorta the cap'n of this bunch. We been hearin' you folks're in a kinda bad time, with yer trade an' all. So we thought we'd come an' see.'

'Real bad time,' said the squat Duster with the big moustache, whose name, Jonmac recalled, was Wace. 'Wipe-out time, seems.'

Robett had not changed expression. 'Where would you hear a thing like that?'

'Stiks, friend,' said the Duster leader, Strake. 'We got so's we can talk to 'em a bit. They say yer done for, tradin' here. Say they won't come near you again.'

Jonmac's stomach seemed to sink into his boots at those words. The others looked shocked and upset – except for big Tranter, who just looked angry.

'That's garbage,' Tranter growled. 'You bringin' a buncha lies to try an' make us leave?'

The moustached Duster, Wace, scowled at him. 'Watch what you say 'bout lies, fella. We got no need to lie. Yer finished on this planet – so you might as *well* leave.'

As the EXTRA team all began to speak at once, Strake's bass voice rose above them. 'Wace here, he says things kinda blunt, but that's how it is. Stiks say you folks did 'em wrong somehow. Broke one of their laws or somethin'. So they're done with you fer good. You won't see 'em again.'

'So time to get goin',' Wace added, with an ugly laugh. 'Buncha pikers. Come inta space with yer little vibe-guns, think you know it all, think EXTRA's runnin' things. This time, pikers, yer just *runnin'*.'

Jonmac saw cold fury flame in the eyes of Coln Robett, saw big Tranter's fists bunch, saw his mother's face turn white with anger. And the Dusters saw those reactions too, and laughed.

'Like I said,' Strake rumbled, 'Wace's kinda blunt. Time fer you EXTRAS to pack up an' lift off. This world's a write-off fer you, now.'

'We could help 'em,' Wace said, lifting his flamer with a grin. 'Burn some of these little pre-fabs. Save packin' 'em up.'

'You wouldn't dare!' Su said hotly.

'Wouldn't I?' Wace's grin widened. 'How would you stop me, lady? Slap my face with yer *vibe*?'

'Not with a vibe,' Tranter growled.

And he took a long stride forward and punched the Duster in the face.

The movement was quicker than anyone would have expected from such a big man, and the blow was ferocious. Wace was flung backwards, his face flowering with blood and broken teeth, crumpling unconscious to the ground.

But then the other Dusters were furiously unslinging their weapons. And Strake, face twisting with rage, brought the muzzle of his flamer up to point directly between the eyes of Coln Robett.

7

Everyone went very still, like a vid-tape stopped in freeze-frame. Nothing showed on Robett's face as he locked his gaze unblinkingly on to Strake, as if the flamer did not exist. And at last, slowly, Strake grunted and lowered his weapon, gesturing to his men to do the same.

'That's good sense,' Robett said calmly. 'You've no need to use your flamers.'

'Nothin'' to stop us if we wanted,' Strake rumbled.

Robett's gaze remained unwavering. 'You should know, Strake, that we sent a message to EXTRA about you being here.'

Strake grinned mirthlessly. 'That s'posed to scare me, fella? You think I don't know how long it'd take any more EXTRA folk to get here?' The grin faded. 'I reckon you'll be takin' off, before then, now yer trade's finished. At least, you *better* take off. If you got any of that *good sense* you were talkin' about.'

He turned then, growling at the other Dusters to pick up the still unconscious Wace. And they all swaggered away, leaving behind a final burst of mocking laughter.

Robett looked around at the others, smiling a little at Tranter's sheepish expression.

'Sorry about that,' Tranter muttered. 'Couldn't help myself.'

'He had it coming!' Su said fiercely.

Robett shrugged. 'It was a good punch. And

I don't think there was any real danger of them using their flamers.'

'They had no *need* to,' Loysel snapped. 'If what they say is true – if one of us *has* antagonized the Stiks – then we might as well do as they say, pack up and leave.'

Robett nodded briefly. 'Perhaps. *If* it's true.' He looked around at them all again. 'Can anyone shed any light on this?'

The others looked doubtful or troubled or bewildered in various combinations. But then Su glanced at Jonmac, and saw with a mother's knowledge of her child the quite different turmoil of feelings that showed on his face.

Her eyes widened. 'Jonnie?'

Jonmac felt his insides go empty, his mouth go dry, his eyes begin to prickle with unshed tears. The worst moment of his life had arrived, and there was nothing for him to do but get it over with.

'Yes,' he said in an indistinct mumble. 'It was me. I did . . . what they said.'

Slowly, haltingly, he told them all about it – his discovery of the strange bare clearing with the Stik statues, his dreams of glory, the violent reaction of the Stiks. By the end his voice was stronger, as if unburdening himself of the shameful secret was making him feel better. But even so his face was bloodlessly pale and his hands were trembling slightly.

When he finished, they all simply stared at him for a long silent moment. But he was looking only at Su, seeing the shock and dismay on her face.

'I'm sorry,' he said desperately. 'I know I've . . . ruined everything. But I didn't mean to . . .' He swallowed hard, fighting the tears. 'I don't want you to hate me . . .'

'Oh, Jonnie.' Su put her arms around him in a fierce hug. 'I don't hate you. No one hates you. It was an accident – a lot of rotten, unhappy bad luck. And you might have been killed!'

'That's right, Jonmac,' Chani said sympathetically. 'You mustn't feel so badly. Any one of us might have stumbled on the statues . . .'

'And might have acted the same way,' Barranni agreed.

Ndira nodded. 'It was like an accident waiting to happen.'

'Should've happened to that Wace,' Tranter growled. 'Specially the clout with the axe.'

'The fact is,' Loysel broke in snappishly, 'this shows the foolishness of allowing *children* on these operations. One moment of childish stupidity, and now we have to close everything down and leave, and who *knows* what EXTRA will . . .'

'Loysel, *shut up*.' Coln Robett's voice cut across the flow of words like a blade, silencing him.

Jonmac turned away from Su and the others, lifting his head to meet the steady gaze of his team leader. For a moment Robett's pale eyes seemed to drill into the core of Jonmac's being, weighing and assessing. After a moment, he gave a small nod, and Jonmac felt as if he had passed some crucial test.

'I'm glad you told us, Jonmac,' Robett said. 'Now we know the problem, we can try to do something about it.' Loysel seemed about to speak, but a steely look from Robett closed his mouth. 'And one really interesting thing,' Robett went on, 'is that Jonmac has such a loyal friend . . . What's she called?'

66

'Rikil,' Jonmac said.

Robett nodded. 'I don't think we have paid much attention to Rikil, or to what was happening.'

As most of the others looked puzzled, Su frowned thoughtfully. 'That's true. We joked about Jonnie's little friend, without seeing what was happening or taking it seriously.'

'What're you saying?' Ndira asked.

'Jonmac has made a Stik *friend*,' Robett emphasized. 'They not only communicate, they have a relationship. That's rare enough between a human and an alien. But now it turns out they're close enough for her to *protect* him. To *defend* him, against her own people, after he broke a taboo.'

The others looked startled as they understood. 'You're right,' Chani said wonderingly. 'That's almost unheard of.'

'I wish I could thank Rikil,' Su said.

'I wish you could, too,' Robett said. 'Because she might help us as well. She might tell us how we could try to make amends, to rebuild trust among the Stiks.'

'Then why not just go find her and ask her?' Barranni said.

That led them all to adjourn to the mess hall, where they had their midday meal and went on talking. In the end, though, they knew they could do nothing more than keep trying to make contact with the Stiks – especially Rikil and her family group, if possible. To offer apologies, reassurances, gifts, whatever it took to regain the aliens' trust.

'Don't you think I should go out with one of the groups,' Jonmac asked Robett, 'to look for Rikil?'

Robett shook his head. 'Rikil warned you away

– most likely because some Stiks might still attack you for what you did. So you stay on the base.'

'And get on with your schoolwork,' Su added firmly, and everyone laughed at the heaviness of his sigh.

'In my view,' Loysel said dismissively, 'it will all be a waste of time. Wandering around looking for a lot of superstitious savages, so we can *apologize* to them. They might even *attack* us, when we're in the bush.'

'Never mind, Loy-boy,' Barranni said with a smile. 'You can stay behind, nice and safe.'

'That's not the point . . . !' Loysel spluttered.

'The point,' Tranter said, 'is that we gotta do *somethin'*. We can't just crawl away an' hand over the planet to the Dusters.'

'As far as I can see,' Loysel sniffed, 'they've already got it.'

In the long days that followed, it seemed that Loysel was right. None of the team saw the smallest glimpse of a Stik, anywhere. A group of them, with Su always among them, went out every day and searched the forest, but to no avail. They sometimes felt that they were being watched, but the silent aliens never showed themselves.

Only once did a group of searchers have an encounter in the bush, during those days. Not with Stiks, but with Dusters.

As the group told the others, that evening, they had been roaming out near the big pool where Jonmac had first seen the Dusters. And Dusters were there again, including the moustached Wace, whom Tranter had punched. The group had tried to duck back behind a thicket, out of sight, but twigs had crackled and they were spotted.

'Look – it's the pikers!' one of the Dusters had shouted.

'Ain't you left yet?' another one mocked. 'Don't you know when yer finished?'

'They're finished *now*, is when!' Wace had yelled. And he brought his flamer up and fired.

He was shooting at Tranter, his particular enemy, and perhaps his rage disturbed his aim. The heat-bolt struck a tree just beside Tranter's head – and before Wace could fire again the EXTRA group fled, with Tranter swearing colourfully at every step.

They were not pursued, except by some shouted obscenities and laughter. But the group was shaken enough to return to the base at once. That led Loysel to insist again that staying on the planet was pointless, costly and dangerous. By then one or two of the others were starting to agree with him.

And then Loysel produced what he clearly thought was a brilliant idea.

'We have a real opportunity,' he said briskly, smiling with self-satisfaction. 'There wouldn't be any problems from EXTRA about us leaving here, because we don't have to leave empty-handed.'

Ndira frowned. 'We wouldn't. We'd have the ki-cloth that we've got so far.'

'Which is not a lot,' Barranni muttered.

Loysel's smug smile widened. 'Right, we don't have a lot of cloth. Maybe not enough to cover our running costs. But there is a way we *can* cover those costs, and more. A way to make our *fortunes* – and to be seen by EXTRA not as failures but heroes.'

Jonmac was the first to guess what he was going to say. As he drew in a breath, trying to find the words to express his outrage, Loysel made his meaning clear.

'What we do is load up, get all ready to lift off. Then— ' he smiled triumphantly around at them all – 'we go and grab as many of those *statues* as we can carry, load them up, and go.'

They all looked startled, but some of them also looked interested. As if they felt that it wasn't such a bad idea.

'You can't!' Jonmac cried, anger making his voice rise into a squeak. 'The Stiks . . .'

Loysel waved his hand as if brushing the word away. 'The Stiks don't matter. EXTRA's rules about not offending the natives, not breaking taboos and all that, are set out to protect the *trade*. Keep the natives happy so they keep *trading*. But our trade is finished here, and we're surely leaving anyway. What does it matter if we upset a few *savages*? We'll never see this world again. And the Stiks aren't going to invent spaceflight in a week and chase after us.'

A silence fell as they all looked at each other, wondering and pondering. And Jonmac watched them with furious astonishment.

'You *can't*!' he said again. 'The Stiks made us welcome here! They were our friends!'

'They're not makin' us welcome now,' Tranter pointed out.

'And you're the only one who really got *friendly* with them, Jonmac,' Pheng said.

Su looked worriedly at Jonmac, then at the others. 'I understand how Jonnie feels. It doesn't seem right, somehow . . .'

'It's *stealing*!' Jonmac said fiercely. 'And the

statues must be *precious* to them . . .'

'They'd be precious to us, too,' Loysel said quickly. 'They would make us very rich.'

'And the Stiks could always carve more,' Parria put in. 'What do you think, Coln?'

Robett nodded consideringly. 'All that's true enough.'

Jonmac stared at him, appalled. 'But . . .' he began. Then he stopped as Robett held up a hand.

'That's what I was going to say,' Robett went on. '*But*. Alien art is worth a fortune, as we know. *But* – all of it that is in circulation, on Earth or on colony worlds, has been acquired by *trading*.'

Loysel pursed his lips but said nothing, unable to deny the truth that every space-trader knew.

'And don't forget the anti-trade people,' Robett continued. 'The Alien Protection Committees and the rest. They never stop looking for ways to tie us up with more regulations, or shut us down entirely. That's why EXTRA trains us to be so careful with aliens, to keep everything fair and proper and aboveboard.'

'And why we can't take the statues,' Su said quietly.

Robett nodded. 'The committees would call it looting. Or pillaging, or plundering. They use words like that about our ordinary trade, as it is. We can't show up with art objects that really *were* stolen.'

'How would anyone know?' Loysel asked.

'It would get out,' Robett told him. 'Things like that always do. People might wonder why we ended the ki-cloth trade and left the planet so abruptly. They could work it out from there.'

'Dusters might tell on us, too,' Tranter said.

'I still think . . .' Loysel began. But as he saw that the others were nodding in agreement with Robett, he subsided.

'Let's go on as we are for a few more days,' Robett said. 'Keep trying hard to contact the Stiks. If nothing happens, we'll start to think about leaving.'

Ndira sighed. 'For a moment there I could see myself being a rich lady back on Earth.'

'A rich looter, you would've been,' Barranni said with a laugh. 'Better be poor and honest.'

More empty days followed – days of fruitless searching in the forest, days of disappointment and frustration made worse by Loysel's complaints. For Jonmac, the relief he gained from confessing proved short-lived. By day, he too fell back into gloom and depression, still weighed down by the guilt of being responsible for the trouble. By night, he had a recurring nightmare in which he was alone in the bare clearing where the statues stood when the statues came terrifyingly to life and took ghastly revenge on him for his trespass.

After more than a week of such days and nights, Jonmac rose early on a rain-grey morning, before Su was awake, before anyone was stirring on the base. Restlessly he crept outside, feeling that the clammy air and the dampening mist-fine rain suited his mood perfectly. He wandered aimlessly along the edge of the clearing where the base stood, staring into the shadowed thickets, until he came at last to where the starship rested.

He did not even want to look at the great ship, which seemed to crouch on its undercarriage, ready to spring into the sky. He did not want the reminder that all too soon the ship *would* be leaping away, taking them all off the planet where they had failed – because of him.

He moved past the ship, his mood darkening further. In that morose moment he felt indifferent to the warnings he had been given, the risk that he might be taking if he left the base. Let the Stiks do what they want, he thought bleakly. I probably deserve it.

And he walked away from the base into the bush, circling around a large thicket beyond the ship, his steps almost silent in the rain-sodden undergrowth.

Since his self-pitying gaze was directed downwards, he only sensed that something stood in his way, before he saw anything. But then he looked up with a jolt of shock, gave a strangled cry and stumbled back, almost falling.

Silent and dark and huge, a number of Stiks loomed over him, their spears and axes raised, blades glistening in the rain.

8

He was sure that he was going to die, that the
spears and axes would fall on him. But instead
the Stiks lowered their weapons and did nothing, except regard him steadily. Jonmac dazedly
realized that it was Rikil's family group, who had
been as startled by his sudden appearance around
the thicket as he had been by theirs.

But then delight pushed aside all other feelings, as he saw the small yellow-furred form of
his friend move forward from the midst of the
Stiks.

'Onnak,' Rikil said, her eyes dark and grave.

Jonmac was so happy to see her that he wanted
to shout for joy. But the calm silence of the Stiks
was contagious, and he clutched at his feelings,
reining them in.

'Rikil,' he said. *'Nik'littin, nik'littin.'*

Saying the Stik for 'welcome' twice let her know
how very welcome she was. He saw the flash of
brightness in her eyes and knew that she, too,
was glad to see him again.

'Onnak,' she said again. 'Stikessi come to talk.'

Elation filled Jonmac as he understood. They
might want to start trading again, he thought with
wild hope. But then he flinched as one of the
tallest of the Stiks made a sharp gesture. That Stik
was the family-group leader, named Ilinit, as Rikil
had once told him. And the gesture was clearly
a silencing order, for Rikil at once stepped back,
saying no more.

'We come to talk with Kol,' said the leader, Ilinit, in his own language.

That made Jonmac step back as well. Clearly Ilinit meant that they were there to talk to Coln Roberts, the humans' leader. Not to a child, and certainly not to one who had offended them. In any case, the Stiks then simply marched past Jonmac, on to the base, halting in the middle of the open area. Jonmac heard startled, muffled shouts from inside the buildings as the visitors were noticed. A moment later, the EXTRA team began spilling out, looking variously nervous, wary, pleased and still half asleep.

The Stik leader, Ilinit, then spoke at some length to Coln Robett, with Su at his side intently trying to follow the flow of talk. Jonmac was trying hard to follow it himself, as he stood on the edge of the gathering.

He winced when he heard Ilinit refer to 'the place of bare earth'. But then he had expected that his trespass would be what they were talking about. What if they were there to demand some compensation? Or to demand that Jonmac be punished? Or . . .

He tore himself away from that frightening train of thought. By then Ilinit had stopped talking, and Su was quietly relaying a translation to Robett, as best she could. In that lull, Jonmac tried to put together his own translation. But there had been too many words he had never heard. At last he turned to Rikil, standing silently beside him.

'What did he say?' he asked. Then, remembering one phrase that the Stik leader had used several times, he tried a more specific question. 'What is *rirrik tiss*?'

Rikil repeated the phrase, pronouncing it cor-rectly. 'Like Rikil,' she told him. 'Like Onnak.' She made a gesture, holding her narrow hand up at the height of their heads.

'Short?' Jonmac asked, puzzled. Then light dawned. 'You mean *young*?'

'Young.' Rikil tasted the human word. 'Not many years,' she added, in her own language.

Jonmac nodded, just as Robett was nodding at Su's murmured translation, both of them looking relieved and pleased. Su then said a few halting words in the Stik tongue, gesturing to Robett as if to say they were the words of the human leader. The Stiks listened politely, then spoke among themselves, too quietly and quickly for Jonmac to understand.

At last Ilinit turned back to Robett, gesturing with a long finger up at the sun, which was trying to push some watery light through the rainclouds.

'Stikessi will come back,' he said, '*s'kihir*.' His sweeping gesture showed the word's meaning – one turning of the sun. 'Stikessi will come with *t'kii*. As it was before.'

Without another word, the Stiks then strode away, leaving a group of astonished and delighted humans staring after them.

Rikil held back a moment. 'Rikil will come to Onnak,' she said. '*S'kihir*.'

In his pure delight Jonmac managed to make a complete botch of the Stik gesture that meant 'yes'. That earned him some of the hum that was Rikil's laughter, as she turned away to follow her family-group. But then she looked back, at the edge of the base, and for the first time in what seemed like an eternity she touched her brow and reached out her fluttering hand towards him.

Blinking back a sudden sting in his eyes, Jonmac took a chance – that the movement really was a sign of friendship – and clumsily tried to return it. That earned him another burst of soft laughter as Rikil drifted away into the bush.

In that time the EXTRA group had been erupting in a confused babble of questions and exclamations, but Robett finally managed to quieten them so that Su could explain.

'We've been forgiven,' she said simply. 'These people, who Loysel called *savages*, have been big-hearted enough to forgive us for what happened.'

As Loysel managed a wordless half-sneer, Robett grinned around at them all. 'And they're starting up the trade again. From tomorrow.'

'I'm not complaining,' Ndira said, 'but how come? What's made them so forgiving?'

'Maybe it's their nature,' Chani Pheng said quietly.

Su nodded. 'Maybe. And I think Jonnie's friend, Rikil, had something to do with it.' She glanced over at Jonmac with a smile. 'The leader, who did the talking, said that they realized that the human who intruded on to the place of the statues was still only young, and knew no better. They now understood that he meant no harm, and in fact did no harm. We're still forbidden to go near the statues – but we're forgiven.' Her smile grew wry. 'As far as I could make out, the Stiks feel that we should be forgiven because we *all* know no better. As if we're all like children in some way. The Stik leader said, more or less, that we might know about metal and glass and flying to the stars and things. But we know nothing at all about anything *important*.'

'He may have a point,' Dr Pheng said with a smile. 'But now at least we can go on learning.'

'And trading,' Barranni added.

'The Stik say anythin' about the Dusters?' Tranter asked.

'Not a thing,' Su said. 'But we can be sure that those Stiks, at least, still disapprove of the dust. So maybe others do, too.'

'The Dusters will hate that,' Ndira said lightly, raising a fairly uneasy laugh as they all trooped away for breakfast.

So normality was restored, more or less, as Stiks – a few other small family-groups besides Rikil's – began to return to the EXTRA base. They did not arrive in great numbers, nor with much ki-cloth, but they arrived. During that resumed trade, the team heard occasional news of their rivals, the Dusters. Much of it came from Rikil to Jonmac, who was being taken more seriously as a valuable contact with the aliens. And what he learned was not pleasant, though it may have been predictable.

It seemed that the Dusters had not learned, not immediately, that relations had been restored with the EXTRA team. So, thinking they were still sole masters of the ki-cloth trade, the Dusters grew more arrogant. They demanded far more cloth in exchange for the same small amounts of easy-dust. And they backed up those demands by growing ever more bullying and threatening, at times even vicious and violent.

One day, Rikil told an especially distressing tale. After a trading session with some addicted

Stiks, the Dusters – for the cruel fun of it – had tried to make the Stiks give up their weapons and their ki-cloth garments for more dust. At first the Stiks refused, for it would be a great dishonour, Rikil said. Then the Dusters tried to take the weapons and clothing by force. When some Stiks resisted, the Dusters used their flamers – firing just past and around the Stiks, not to kill but to terrorize. Of course the Stiks fled in panic, some of them suffering burns when the flamer blasts ignited their garments.

The ugliness of the story shocked the EXTRA team when Jonmac related it to another gathering in the mess hall. Everyone looked grim and angry, while Tranter clenched his huge fists till the knuckles went white.

'I hate that,' Tranter growled. 'Stiks don't deserve stuff like that. I really wish we could do somethin' . . .'

'If it happened,' Loysel said with a sniff. 'If it's not some *youthful* exaggeration. Or mistranslation.'

Jonmac felt himself flush. 'It's true!' he said hotly. 'Rikil wouldn't lie. And I understood well enough.'

Loysel sniffed again, but said no more as several of the others glared at him.

'I wish we could do something, too,' Su said. 'Because it's getting worse. The Stiks have spoken of a great many of them who are very sick, perhaps dying, because of what the dust does to them.'

'No doubt,' Dr Pheng said unhappily. 'I imagine the addicts will suffer damage to their breathing, above all.'

'That stuff's bad for *anyone's* breathing,' Ndira said.

'So maybe that'll end up drivin' the Stiks away from the Dusters, after all,' Tranter said hopefully. 'Drivin' them here.'

'Not likely,' Robett said. 'Most of the Stiks around here have been addicted. They need the dust. So they'll have to trade with the Dusters no matter what they do.'

Tranter scowled. 'I reckon Barranni an' me should find us some Dusters, zap 'em with our vibes, grab their flamers an' go blast the others.'

Robett shook his head wearily. 'We're not soldiers or police, we're traders. If we started a fire-fight, there's no telling where it would end.'

Tranter grimaced, then shrugged. 'Yeah, I know. But there's gotta be *some* way to get rid of 'em.'

'It's more likely to be the other way around,' Loysel said harshly. 'When the Dusters know we're trading again, they could start looking for ways to get rid of *us*. And they wouldn't have any scruples about how they'd do it.'

That warning served to make everyone tense all over again. Especially when Robett decided to set a regular watch, day and night, on the base. Still, nothing unusual happened. The days passed, with a few friendly Stiks arriving to trade now and then, and although that didn't enlarge the team's store of ki-cloth by much, it was better than nothing.

Otherwise, everyone stayed on the base, or moved with great caution into the forest if their scientific work required it. For they all knew that it was only a matter of time before the

Dusters learned that the EXTRA team was still there.

But none of them could have guessed how the Dusters would react, when they did find out.

The bad news came first not from Rikil but from the family-group leader, Ilinit, talking to Su and Robett. Apparently Ilinit and his group had been spotted, by some dust-addicted Stiks, heading to the EXTRA base with armloads of ki-cloth. There was every chance that the addicts would hurry to the Dusters with the news, hoping for an easy-dust reward.

'That's *it*,' Loysel said, when everyone had been told the news. 'It'll be *war*, now.'

'I don't think Strake is stupid enough to come shooting,' Robett replied.

Tranter glowered. 'Maybe we oughta try my idea.'

'Count me in,' Barranni said.

Robett shook his head. 'I said before, we're not going to start anything. I can't believe the Dusters will see us as much of a threat to their trade.'

'Better keep our heads down, all the same,' Tranter growled. ''Cause I don't think that gun-happy Wace character, for one, is gonna be pleased we're still here.'

That thought, and the awareness of ruthless and violent enemies lurking not too far away, did nothing for the level of nervous tension on the base. Over the next few days the team tended to stay inside their buildings. If they had to move from one to another, they scuttled quickly with shoulders hunched, in case snipers waited in the forest to pick them off. Trading with passing Stiks was particularly nerve-racking, since the

81

aliens would not enter a building but insisted on remaining in the open.

All the same, as before, while the level of alarm and stress rose, nothing happened. Days went by, and then more days, without any sign of Dusters anywhere nearby. Slowly the team began to relax a little, despite Robett's reminders of the need for care and alertness.

But all relaxation abruptly ended for the team, on another day, when a small group of Stiks, not Rikil's group, came to trade. The Stiks passed by a cluster of thorny shrubs near the edge of the base. And there they paused – and did something terrible, something that the humans had never known Stiks to do.

They screamed.

It was actually more of a rasping howl, the sound that came from them. As they howled, they began to tremble and sway, clutching at each other. As if they had all been suddenly afflicted, together, by some dire agony or illness.

Jonmac and Su had been near to that side of the base. So as all the humans rushed to find out what was wrong, the two of them were the first to see the cause of the aliens' outcry. But only Jonmac recognized that cause. Because he was the only one of the team to have seen its like before.

As the Stiks continued to howl and shake in their apparent pain, one of them stooped jerkily down from his great height and picked something up. Something that had been lying unseen among the shrubs until the Stiks discovered it.

The howling grew even more agonized – accompanied, then, by a wild brandishing of spears and axes – as the Stik straightened with the object in his arms.

The unmistakeable, gleaming shape of one of the statues from the forbidden clearing.

9

Fear gripped Jonmac with icy fingers as he watched the howling aliens gather around the statue, reaching out to touch it, their voices growing more shrill. The statue seemed to be one of the smaller ones from the clearing, looking delicate and fragile. And it had strange flexible extensions jutting from its feet, like roots – which was obviously what held the statues so firmly upright on the ground.

Some of those long slim tendrils had been broken off, Jonmac saw, when the statue had been forcibly removed. To be placed beside the base, so the EXTRA team would be blamed.

Of course the Dusters had done it. Jonmac had no doubt. They had probably learned about the statues from some addicts, and saw an ideal way to discredit the EXTRA team. But there was no chance that the Stiks would believe that explanation, or even listen to it. They seemed almost out of their minds, still howling and shaking. And by then they were also shaking their axes and spears at the humans, threateningly, so that some of the team had reached for their vibes.

But in the end the Stiks all suddenly wheeled away, lurching as if their frenzy affected their balance. Carrying the pathetic little statue, they stumbled into the forest, far more noisily than usual, the crackling of branches accompanying their continuing cries. And then they were gone, though their sounds faded more slowly.

'Well, now,' Tranter said heavily. 'Thought for sure they were comin' at us.'

'Would've bet on it,' Barranni agreed.

They moved slowly away, all together, heading for the mess hall where they always gathered. And there they sat, at first in silence, as if the strength of the Stik emotions had overwhelmed them. In the end it was Ndira who put into words what was in all their minds.

'So the Dusters have found a real good way to get rid of us,' she said dourly.

Robett rubbed a hand across his eyes, then glanced around. 'Any chance it *wasn't* the Dusters?'

'I hope you don't think any of *us* took the thing,' Loysel snapped.

'We'd have hidden it better,' Barranni said with a humourless laugh, as all the others asserted their innocence.

Robett nodded. 'It had to be asked. Anyway, as Ndira said, the Dusters have really done it. I can't see us ever regaining the Stiks' trust – not after the way they reacted out there.'

'No,' Su said miserably. 'It was terrible. I've never seen them like that before.'

'We've never seen 'em that *mad* before,' Tranter said.

'It wasn't just anger.' Su was staring into emptiness, her eyes shadowed in her pale face. 'Something else made them cry out like that, and lose their balance and everything. As if they were . . . *grieving*.'

'They probably were,' Chani suggested. 'If they see the statues as religious or sacred objects. They'd see the removal of a statue as not just vandalism, but *desecration* of a holy thing.'

'Exactly,' Parria agreed. 'It looked like they went into deep shock, which might certainly cause loss of balance along with the howling and everything.'

Robett held up a hand. 'Put it all in some reports, if you like. Right now, it's the anger that matters most. How long it'll last, if it'll get worse, what it'll make them do. Those are the important questions at the moment.'

'Wouldn't bet on them gettin' over it too fast,' Tranter growled.

'No,' Robett agreed grimly. 'So we keep on taking precautions. We stay on the base, we maintain the watch, and we stay alert.'

Loysel sniffed. 'We can be as alert as we like, but you know the Stiks move like *ghosts* in the bush.'

'Have to come out of the bush to get at us,' Barranni pointed out.

'So it'd be kinda good if somebody saw 'em comin',' Tranter added.

That might once have produced a laugh, but no one could manage even a small smile in that meeting.

'It might help,' Robett continued, 'if we stay away from the edge of the base. We'll pull back, move everything into the buildings nearest the ship, so we're not scattered. And we'd better sleep on the ship at night.'

As the others groaned, thinking of the cramped conditions they would be facing, Loysel looked very disapproving. 'It would be more sensible if we simply left the planet,' he announced.

'We probably will,' Robett replied, startling Loysel. 'But not too hastily. As long as we can stay on guard and keep ourselves safe, I'd rather

86

stay around for a little while and see what happens.'

'What *more* could happen?' Loysel demanded.

'You never know, Loy boy,' Tranter said, with a wink at Barranni. 'Stiks might all move to the other side of the planet.'

'Or a meteor might fall,' Barranni said, 'on top of all the Dusters.'

As Loysel began to splutter, Parria raised her voice to be heard. 'You don't think the Stiks will come round to *forgive* us, like before, Coln? Because I don't think so. This isn't just a little intrusion – it's a desecration, like Chani said.'

'I know,' Robett said patiently. 'But I also know we didn't do it. If we give it a little time, the Stiks might find that out.'

'How?' Loysel scoffed. 'The Dusters aren't likely to *confess*.'

Robett shrugged. 'I've no idea how, yet. But it could happen. As long as we feel fairly safe, we should stay awhile and see.'

'I agree,' Su said firmly, and most of the others slowly added their assent.

'One thing might happen,' Dr Pheng said. 'The Dusters might get more greedy as well as arrogant. They might try to take more statues, for themselves. *Then* the Stiks would know.'

'I'll tell you what *I* know,' Loysel said bitterly. 'As surely as I know anything. If we stay here any longer, we'll *regret* it!'

'Thanks for that, Loy,' Ndira said acidly. 'If the Stiks come and kill us all, we'll have to remember that you told us so.'

From then on the EXTRA team began another sequence of days filled with unending tension and

87

watchfulness, combined with a sense of something unknown but ominous advancing steadily towards them. But for Jonmac, things had changed.

He was no longer suffering his previous misery and guilt, for those had melted away with the Stiks' forgiveness and Rikil's return. Instead, he was immersed in feelings of *loss*. When the Stiks had first returned, Jonmac had realized just how important to him Rikil's friendship was. Now, through no fault of theirs, they had been separated again, their unusual relationship probably cut off forever.

If the team had to leave the planet, he would never see Rikil again. The thought troubled him greatly in those days. He longed to see her, to talk with her, to explain everything to her. At the very least, he did not want to go without saying goodbye.

But he was stuck on the base, with nothing to do except go through the motions of schoolwork or watch vid-films or vid-books, most of which he had already viewed. He wasn't even allowed to take his turn on watch, being deemed too young, which annoyed him greatly.

So while the rest of them were being watchful and often fearful, Jonmac was feeling too sad and generally too restless to care about wariness and fear.

His restlessness was not helped by spending nights on the ship, as Robett had ordered. Living quarters on a cruiser-class starship, one of the smaller classes that could land on a planet, were as painfully cramped as those of the ancient seafarers that Jonmac had studied in history. Narrow, spartan bunks, the men jammed in one cell-like cabin and the women in another.

On an actual flight, the team would have taken the FTL drugs that made faster-than-light travel bearable. They would have slept much of the time and been tranquillized into near-zombies when awake. So in flight they would barely notice the conditions. But spending nights that way on land, without drugs, was another matter.

Nor were things much better on the base by day. As Robett had directed, everyone had moved their things into the two buildings closest to the ship, so as not to be scattered and vulnerable. So those two buildings became like the ship – cramped and uncomfortable, cluttered with everyone's belongings and equipment.

Everyone tried to find a corner of their own to work in during the day. But they were all too aware of discomfort and danger to get much done. As nerves grew more raw, the members of the team began to avoid each other more, seeking some moments of privacy. And Jonmac, edgy and fretful as the rest of them, did the same.

Whenever he could, he slipped outside and wandered around the base in the cool fresh air, until he was sent back in by whomever was on watch. Sometimes, though, he managed to keep out of sight for some while. And then, just to ease his boredom and reduce his gloom, he would do exactly what he was not supposed to do.

He would drift quietly over to one of the now-deserted buildings on the outer edge of the base, farthest from the ship. And there, safely inside, he would stare moodily and longingly into the depths of the forest. Wishing that somehow he would one day see the Stiks emerging, to say that they had earned the truth and all was well again. With Rikil among them, returning to her friend.

But it never happened, as the days went on and on.

Eventually the team began the first stages of closing down the base. They loaded all the ki-cloth on to the ship, they carefully packed away much of their equipment, furnishings and so on. And the finality of all that made Jonmac even gloomier.

Until a day when gloom and tension and fear gave way to something unimaginably worse.

Another fine misty rain was falling on that day, but despite it Jonmac drifted outside again, in the late afternoon. He saw that Loysel was on watch, and waited for a chance to slip past the little man and get to his usual station, in the mostly empty building farthest from the ship.

In its emptiness the place seemed more doleful than ever. And outside there was nothing to see in the fading light, as dusk approached. Only rain-wet scrawny branches that seemed to be gathering and holding the fine mist in armfuls.

But from a side window there was something to see, if not very interesting. Just Loysel, clutching his vibe-gun in his hand as if he was a real sentry. The little man was near the edge of the base, turning his head this way and that as if looking for something. Maybe for me, Jonmac thought, with a twinge of worry that his secret visits to the outer building might be discovered.

He watched Loysel steadily, ready to duck out if the little man started towards the building. But Loysel stayed where he was, looking oddly tense as he stared around at the darkening bush. Maybe he heard one of the big bugs, Jonmac thought. He's probably scared of them.

That made him smile a little, knowing how harmless the creatures were. He was still smiling when he saw a dark object flit soundlessly through the air, towards Loysel's back, looking very like a flying creature.

Loysel shrieked, staggered, dropped the vibe and fell to the ground.

Jonmac stared, stunned. Loysel was thrashing on the ground, wailing thinly like a terrified child. In the dimness Jonmac couldn't see what it was that had hit him – but he could see the dark spreading redness around Loysel's writhing body.

That's *blood*, he thought dazedly. Loysel's *hurt*.

He began to turn to the door, hearing from across the base the voices of the others in the team as they came to Loysel's aid. But before he turned fully away from the window, he glimpsed another of the dark shadows flash through the air, outside, towards Loysel.

It flew in a higher arc than the first one, and landed differently, so he could see more clearly just what it was.

A Stik spear – its dagger-sharp head stabbing deep into the ground less than a stride from where Loysel lay.

10

Stricken with fright, hardly able to believe what he had seen, Jonmac stared from his window as the EXTRA team rushed into view, drawn by Loysel's cries. They were met by a terrifying shower of spears and axes, hurtling out of the mist-filled brush. The weapons fell short, but made the humans back quickly away, trying to find protection behind the nearest building.

Jonmac heard his mother call out something in the Stik language, no doubt pleading with them to stop. Her answer was another few spears, striking into the ground near the team's position. As yet none of the alien attackers had showed themselves, nor had they made any sound within the bush around the base. Meanwhile Loysel's cries were fading to whimpers, the pool of redness spreading around him.

The EXTRA team had a quick huddled discussion. Then from their midst burst big Tranter, moving in a crouch at a considerable pace. A spear or two flew towards him as he ran, but missed. He reached Loysel and stooped down to the little man.

The stoop saved his life. A white-hot stream of energy blasted through the air where his head had been. A blast from a flamer.

'*Dusters*,' Jonmac whispered aloud.

As the blast of flame missed, and Tranter dropped flat beside Loysel, everyone heard the cry of frustrated fury from the brush. The ugly voice of Wace, raging at his miss.

That was followed by another flurry of spears and axes aimed at the EXTRA team, with more flamer bursts among them. By then Tranter, flat on his belly, was crawling away, dragging Loysel with him, ignoring the spears falling around him and the fiery blasts sizzling above him. The rest of the team were crouched behind their building, their almost useless vibes in their hands, still not having seen any of their attackers.

'Strake!' It was Coln Robett's voice, rising above the noise of battle. 'This is crazy! You'll never get away with it!'

Jonmac jerked as he heard the Duster captain's reply burst out from a thicket almost next to the building where Jonmac was hiding.

'We're *gettin'* away with it!' Strake roared. 'What we got here is a good ol' native uprisin'! You think EXTRA's gonna fly in to yer rescue?'

He punctuated his words with a burst from his flamer, with Wace and the others following suit. Then, for the first time in the attack, Jonmac saw shadowy glimpses of Stiks, creeping slowly forward through the brush. Crouching as they were, long arms trailing, with more spears and axes in their long spidery hands, the mist swirling eerily around them, Jonmac thought they had never looked more alien or more terrifying.

The rest of the team obviously thought so too. 'Move back!' he heard Robett order. 'Get to the ship!'

That brought another wild burst of firing from the Dusters as the EXTRA team sprinted away, trying to keep the buildings between them and the attackers. Flames leaped up as many of the plastishell structures were hit – and smoke poured across the base, making visibility even worse. In that dimness, Jonmac crept to his building's door, shaking with fear, and began slowly to open it.

In front of his face, the door burst into flame.

He flung himself back with a cry, aware that a Duster must have seen the door's movement and fired at it.

'Someone in there, Strake!' he heard a Duster yell. 'I might've got him!'

Jonmac stared around wildly. If he could open one of the windows . . .

He did not have time to try. Through the flames of the doorway leaped a squat, ugly figure, savage grin bright beneath a huge moustache. Wace, with flamer ready.

'Say g'bye, piker,' Wace snarled, and brought the weapon up to fire.

But the searing heat of the blast scorched past Jonmac's shoulder. The big Duster captain, Strake, had lumbered through the doorway to fling Wace aside just as he fired.

'Hold it, Wace,' Strake rumbled. 'It's the kid. We might have a use fer him . . .'

He paused. From over near the starship, they all heard a shrill and anguished cry. Su Lowde's voice, raised in the heart-breaking scream of a mother who has lost her child.

'Jonnnieeee!'

Strake showed no reaction, merely listening to see if the cry would be repeated. But he did not fail to see Jonmac's reaction, the terror and desperation in the boy's eyes.

'You'll be Jonnie, then,' Strake said casually. 'Yep – could be real useful. Wace, bring him.'

He turned and pushed out through the door. By

then the flames were spreading from the charred opening through and over the rest of the building. But Wace took the time to search Jonmac, taking his vibe and the little responder and flinging them into the flames. Then the Duster dragged Jonmac outside.

There he saw that the other buildings of the base were also all aflame. And there was no sign of the EXTRA team.

Strake swore angrily. 'I sure hope nothin' valuable's bein' burned up in there,' he growled. 'Or I'm gonna do some harm to some flame-happy deadbrains.' He stared at Jonmac. 'Boy, where's yer good stuff kept? All yer ki-cloth an' ever'thin'?'

Jonmac thought of refusing to answer, but then realized that there was no need for such heroics. 'On the ship,' he said. 'Nearly everything was loaded up in the last few days.'

He almost smiled as he said it, knowing that the Dusters could not hope to break into a starship, not even with flamers.

Strake scowled. 'So yer folks were gettin' ready to pull out. An' I reckon they're all on the ship theirselves now, feelin' safe.' The scowl altered to an unsettling grin. 'But we got *you*. So we'll see if yer folk feel like some tradin'. See what they'll give, to get you back.'

Wace chortled loudly. 'Great, Strake. Good thing I found him.'

'Good thing I stopped you shootin' him, deadbrain,' Strake rumbled.

By then the rest of the Dusters were straggling over to them, with the Stiks visible at the edge of the forest, silently watching the burning buildings.

'EXTRA folk all got inta their ship,' one of the Dusters reported glumly. 'Stiks mighta got another, we ain't sure.'

Wace spat. 'If they'd surrounded the base an' charged 'em, like we said,' he complained, 'they mighta got 'em all. But they hadda *throw* their spears an' stuff from the bush. Never saw stupider aliens.'

'Yep, kinda stupid,' Strake agreed. 'Didn't help that they were half-blind an' near fallin' over, all that easy-dust they sniffed up. But could be worse. We got the boy, an' he's what we need to get them folks outa their ship.'

The Dusters inspected Jonmac with interest, as if he was a new form of trade goods. Which is just what I am, Jonmac thought shakily, staring past the men at the flames leaping in the ruined buildings.

'We'll take him back to the ship,' Strake went on. 'Have some chow, 'cause all this exercise makes me hungry. Then we'll get the comm goin', an' make a call to *their* ship. An' start tradin'.'

As they all laughed, brutally, Wace's powerful hand clamped on to Jonmac's wrist, dragging him away as the Dusters headed into the darkening forest.

Some hours later, Jonmac was huddled in a corner of an upper-level area in the Dusters' starship, feeling wretched, scared and vaguely sick to his stomach.

All the Dusters were crowded in there as well, in the area that housed the ship's main control area, with all its computer banks, scanner screens and everything. And most of the equipment looked

96

as old, patched-together and poorly maintained as the rest of the ship.

Not that Jonmac had seen the outside of it too clearly. By the time the Dusters had trudged through the brush to the ship, several kilometres from the EXTRA base, full darkness had fallen. But most of them carried small handlights, and in their brightness Jonmac had seen enough. The Duster starship was a cruiser-class like the EXTRA ship, though perhaps an older model, with a hull much stained and scarred. It stood in a small open area that was burned black by the careless down-blast of the landing.

Inside, the ship was messy, dirty, smelly and poorly maintained. The lights were dim, and the recycled air from the life-support system smelled of mould and feet. And the food they had eaten – the basic protein concentrate mixed with unknown, half-rancid vegetable matter – was much of the reason for Jonmac's feelings of nausea.

After washing down their food with some dubious-looking drink, the Dusters had dragged Jonmac into the control area, set him aside, and got on with business. Which seemed to be mostly sniffing their own easy-dust while watching Strake try to contact the EXTRA ship.

Without success. He tried over and over, switching to a range of different frequencies on the ship's communicator, but there was no answer.

'Maybe the atmosphere's cloggin' the transmit,' Nace said.

Strake scowled. 'Could be, in all this dam' foggy bush. Could be the comm's *busted* again.' He slammed a huge hand on the communicator console, then leaned back with a sour grin.

''Course, might be they just don't wanna talk to us. Might be mad at us fer somethin'.'

That brought raucous laughter from the others, except Wace, who frowned. 'They gotta talk to us,' he said. 'We got their kid.'

Strake glanced over at Jonmac. 'Maybe they don't *know* we got him. Maybe they think he got dead back there. Burnt up in one of the buildin's or somethin'.'

'That'll make *them* real burnt up,' one of the men said, cackling at his own wit.

'They might come after us,' another one said, grinning.

'With *vibes*?' Wace asked, and the raucous laughter burst out again.

Strake yawned. 'I don't reckon they'll do that. Not t'night, anyways. So put the kid somewhere an' leave him be. Tomorrow, Wace, you an' a coupla the boys head back over there, talk to their ship direct. Tell 'em we got their Jonnie. Tell 'em I want their boss to come back here with you, so I can give him our terms.'

Two of the others obediently hoisted Jonmac to his feet and half-dragged him away. As they moved through the narrow metal companionways and passages, it was even more clear that the ship was older and scruffier than the EXTRA ship. But Jonmac was too deep in fear and misery to pay much attention to the squalor around him. Not even when the men shoved him through a doorway into what had to be a cargo hold, half-filled with untidy piles of ki-cloth, dimly lit by a tiny permalamp on the ceiling.

'This'll do fer ya, kid,' one of the men told him. 'Use the cloth fer sleepin'.'

The second man glared at Jonmac. 'This door's

got no lock, boy. But don't you even *think* about sneakin' out or nothin'. There's no way off the ship fer you till we take you. An' if we hafta tie you up to keep you in here, you won't like it. Unnerstand?'

Jonmac nodded dully without replying. Satisfied, the Dusters left, slamming the metal door, leaving Jonmac alone. For a moment he simply stood where they left him, staring around at his unlovely prison. Then with a heartsick sigh he sank down on to the ki-cloth, grimacing at its faint, sickly-sweetish odour.

He lay there for a long time without moving. Unstoppably, his mind kept replaying the scenes of the attack – Loysel writhing in his blood, Tranter rescuing the little man under flamer fire, the buildings all ablaze, and finally the sound of his mother's agonized voice, screaming his name. But beyond even those terrible images, his mind kept fixing on the fact that he had been stupidly, disobediently, on the wrong part of the base, in a building where he shouldn't have been.

So he had been exposed to capture. And now the Dusters were going to use him to impose their will on the EXTRA team.

It's all my fault, he thought woefully. Like it was my fault before.

The renewed feelings of guilt and shame made him twist and squirm on the cloth. But what was most unbearable was the thought of how his mother would be feeling right then. Thinking, as Strake believed, that he was dead. Mourning him. But also knowing how much of everything was his fault . . .

For the first time since his capture, alone there in the cargo hold, he stopped fighting the tears that he had held back for so long. Lying in the dimness he curled into a ball and sobbed out his fear and guilt and loneliness – until at last he slid down into an exhausted, dream-scarred sleep.

He awoke with a jerk, for an instant failing to remember where he was. But the grey heaps of ki-cloth around him let him know. He was a prisoner of the Dusters, about to be exchanged for as much as they could get from the EXTRA team.

The light from the permalamp was of course exactly the same, so he had no idea if it was night or day. But he soon found out, when the door of the cargo hold was jerked open by the same two Dusters who had taken him there.

'On yer feet, kid,' one of them said. 'You aim to sleep all day?'

They hustled him out of the room, taking him along towards their quarters and into the tiniest, filthiest washroom that he had ever seen. But he was glad of it, especially when a chipped mirror showed his face grey with ki-cloth dust with trails and blotches left by his tears. He used some tepid water for a quick wash, dried his face with his shirt-tail, then went out to be hustled away again.

They took him back to the main control area where Strake and most of the others were again gathered. Strake looked him over with a grin that was almost a sneer.

'Don't look so miserable, kid,' he rumbled. 'Wace an' some of the boys are over at yer ship. If yer cap'n shows sense in the tradin', you'll be back with yer ma 'fore dark.'

Jonmac remained silent, turning away as the two Dusters took him back to the corner where he had been placed before, out of the way, with a wedge of protein concentrate for breakfast, which he gnawed at half-heartedly. And then they all idled around, waiting.

It turned out not to be too long a wait. It ended when they all heard the sounds that indicated other people were nearby in the ship, coming towards the control area. Jonmac sat up tensely, wondering if Coln Robett would be coming in, and how angry he would be at Jonmac's presence there.

But when Wace and three other Dusters came in, they were alone. No one from the EXTRA team had come back with them.

And the looks they flung in Jonmac's direction were peculiar – mingling a kind of secret, cruel glee with something like surprise.

'What's this?' Strake demanded. 'Don't they wanna trade? Don't they want their boy back? What'd they *say*?'

'Said nothin',' Wace replied, glancing at Jonmac again. ''Cause they ain't *there*, Strake. Their ship's lifted off. They're *gone*.'

PART TWO

MAROONED

11

Wace's words struck Jonmac like invisible clubs. He jerked and gasped, his face ashen, his body turning cold. Suddenly he was on his feet, teeth bared like a maddened animal, leaping at Wace's throat.

'You're *lying*, you're *lying*!' he screeched, fists flailing with wild blows. 'Liar, liar, they *can't* be gone, they *can't* . . .'

For an instant Wace backed away from the unexpected assault. But then he snarled and swung a vicious backhand that smashed into the side of Jonmac's face and flung him sprawling.

'Wace!' Strake rumbled warningly, as the squat man seemed about to pick Jonmac up and hit him again.

'Kid punched me, you see that?' Wace snarled unbelievingly, touching the slight smear of blood from his nose where one of Jonmac's frenzied fists had landed.

'Yer news mighta upset him some,' Strake said dryly.

By then Jonmac was on his feet again, a bruise darkening his cheek, his arms gripped by two Dusters. But the fighting madness seemed to have left him. Sagging in the men's grip, he looked as if intelligence and will and sanity itself were draining away from him, under the awful impact of what he had been told.

The misery and self-blame of the night before were nothing compared to the torrent of agony blasting through him then, in his realization that he had been left behind. Nothing like a sensible thought could form in his mind as desolation and terror howled through him. He saw and heard his surroundings as if from a great distance. And while his mind struggled feebly against the gigantic shock, he could make no sense of what the Dusters were doing or saying.

It may have been just as well. Wace was describing the state of the EXTRA base, where only one or two buildings, he said, remained even partly intact. Even so, Wace said, he and the others had found a few containers of food and even some bits of equipment and furnishings, left behind in the intact buildings. As if the EXTRA team had been in a great hurry to finish loading and lift off, after the attack.

'Some of the food looked OK,' Wace added. 'Better'n what we got.'

Strake grunted. 'We'll go over sometime an' clear ever'thin' out. Anythin' we can use or sell.'

One of the other men gestured at the communicator console. 'You gonna try callin' their ship again, Strake? Tell 'em we got their boy?'

Strake gave the man a withering look. 'Sure, great idea. Put a comm call like that inta space. Where *anybody* could pick it up, even light-years away. Anybody who might be real interested in hearin' 'bout Dusters stealin' EXTRA kids.' He glowered around at the console. 'Even if the dam' comm was workin', I wouldn't call.'

'So what *do* we do?' Wace asked. ''Fore long, those pikers'll be tellin' EXTRA everythin'.'

Strake snorted. 'An' EXTRA will say, well dearie me, ain't that terrible. If they send a force, wouldn't get here in less'n a coupla months or so, soonest. An' we'll be long gone by then.'

'We will?' Wace asked, surprised.

'Yep,' Strake said. 'We spend a coupla weeks or so, now, gettin' the Stiks jumpin', bringin' in all the cloth they can carry an' then some. Keep at it hard, pack the ship full, then go. Then it won't matter if EXTRA sends folks or not.'

All the men seemed to agree with that. 'I was gettin' sick of this bush anyways,' one said.

'An' we stay too long, we gonna run outa dust,' another said.

''Specially the way *you* suck it up,' a third said, and they all laughed.

'What about the kid?' Wace asked, scowling towards Jonmac. 'He's no use to us now. Want me to finish him?'

Everyone turned to stare at Jonmac. But he did not return their gaze, or show any awareness of his new danger – still overcome by his inner agonies of loss and despair.

'Nope,' Strake said at last. 'We keep him.'

'What fer?' Wace demanded. 'What good is he?'

'More'n you think, Wace,' Strake said slowly. ''Cause a deadbrain like you can't look *ahead*, an' see what I'm seein'.'

'What're you seein'?' Wace scoffed.

'I'm seein' what happens when the boy's folks report to EXTRA,' Strake rumbled. 'Their news is gonna make a lotta folks real mad. Not just mad enough to send a little force lookin' fer us. I mean mad enough to make gover'ments, an' everyone, think about gettin' rid of *all* Dusters, anywhere. You wanta trigger off somethin' like that?'

Wace grimaced, with a surly shrug, but some

of the others were looking troubled. 'You think it could happen?' one asked.

'Could,' Strake said. 'Think about it. Up to now, Dusters've just been a nuisance, not much more. Takin' some of EXTRA's trade sometimes, gettin' a little rough now an' then. But never enough to get folks worked up, to get 'em spendin' lotsa time an' cash comin' after us. But now . . .' He stared around at each of them meaningfully. 'These folks who just left from here are gonna tell how we attacked 'em. They won't mention a Stik uprisin', that'd make 'em look bad. No, they'll tell about how we burned their base – an', worst of all, how we killed their young *kid*, their Jonnie . . . That could stir ever'body up. 'Specially if the vid-news an' fax-press get goin' on it. We could have a hard time findin' a place to *hide*, let alone sell our ki-cloth!'

As he paused again, even Wace was looking worried. 'What do we do, then?' one of the men asked, tensely.

Startlingly, Strake grinned. 'We make use of the boy,' he said. 'We show up on Earth soon as we're done here. We get in touch with EXTRA – an' give 'em the boy back, alive. So people are happy, an' things cool down. Along the way we tell a few lies to the vidcasters, tell 'em EXTRA's lyin' 'bout us. We say that there was a scuffle on the planet with the natives, an' the EXTRA folk ran off – leavin' their boy behind! Desertin' him! An' we'll say they're puttin' the blame on us to cover up an' save their face.' He laughed. 'It'll be our word 'gainst theirs, an' EXTRA will want the whole thing to get forgot real quick.'

The men were also grinning by then, even Wace. Also, though they did not notice, Jonmac was slowly lifting his head to stare at Strake. Despite all his inner storms, some of the talk had begun to get through to him. Especially the plan that Strake had just outlined. He cared little for the reasoning behind it – but very much for the plan itself.

They would take him home.

So he began to lift his head, while new hope and yearning sprang up within him, quelling some of the tempest of fear and desolation. And he began to listen more closely, as the Dusters savoured their leader's foresight.

'What about the kid, though?' Wace asked. 'He'll talk too. Tell how we grabbed him an' all . . .'

'Grabbed him?' Strake's grin widened. 'No, no, we *saved* him, got him away from all the attackin' Stiks. Right? An' we were gonna hand him back to his folks, but they just lifted off an' left him. Right?' He glanced at Jonmac, no humour at all showing in his eyes. 'His word 'gainst ours, just like with the others. Nobody can prove nothin'.'

'Yer really somethin', Strake,' one man said admiringly. 'You think of ever'thin'.'

'That's how come I'm cap'n,' Strake rumbled, 'an' a deadbrain like Wace ain't.'

They all laughed uproariously, including Wace himself.

'Now,' Strake told them at last, 'let's get to work.' He fixed Jonmac with a cold gaze. 'Jonnie boy, you'll get looked after, long's you do what yer told. Keep outa the way, don't try to leave the ship, you'll be fine. Make any trouble – you get tied up, you don't eat regular, maybe you get hurt some. Unnerstand?'

For a moment Jonmac met his gaze. Then he looked down, with a small shaky nod.

'Right,' Strake said. 'Won't be long 'fore you're safe home.'

'An' 'fore we're safe on Earth,' another man cackled, 'spendin' all our money!'

Over the days that followed, it was clear that the Dusters were aiming to have a great deal of money to spend. For all their slovenly ways, they could work hard and tirelessly when required. Their ki-cloth trade began to expand like never before.

Jonmac saw none of the trading, though, since he was strictly obeying Strake's orders – doing nothing that might make them change their minds about taking him home. But he overheard enough casual remarks to get the idea of the Dusters' big trading push spreading even wider through the forest, spreading the easy-dust addiction more widely among the Stiks. Ki-cloth poured into the ship, and the cargo holds began to fill up.

By then Jonmac had been moved nearer the men's quarters, into a tiny cubicle that might have been a spare cabin or storeroom. It was entirely bare save for a small heap of ki-cloth tossed on the floor for Jonmac. But it had the small advantage of being closer to the foul washroom that he was allowed to use.

Jonmac spent most of those days sitting or lying on his makeshift bed, sometimes half-dozing, sometimes day-dreaming, but most often almost frantic with boredom as the empty hours inched by. And with the boredom was non-stop tension and worry – that the Dusters might change their plans for him, that something unforeseen might happen.

The tension grew worse still, one evening, when from the passageway outside his cubicle he heard Strake and Wace coming to a fateful decision.

'Nearly there, Wace,' he heard Strake saying as the two men passed by. 'We'll keep on maybe three, four more days. Then just 'fore we pull out, we'll take the boys an' go get some of those statues.'

Jonmac's breath caught in his throat. Yet, he thought, he might have expected it. Of course the Dusters would know how much the statues would be worth. And they would care nothing for how the Stiks might value them, or the Stiks' taboos about them.

At least, Jonmac thought bitterly, when the Dusters stole the statues, the Stiks would learn – too late – that they had been wrong about the EXTRA team.

'Why just *some* of 'em?' Wace was asking.

'Depends how many there are,' Strake said. 'Maybe too many for us to carry. 'Specially if the Stiks try to stop us.'

'They better not,' Wace snarled, and Jonmac could imagine the squat man hefting his flamer. 'Bush'll be fulla roast Stik if they do.'

Strake chuckled unpleasantly. 'Leave 'em somethin' to remember us by.'

'They'll remember us,' Wace said with an equally ugly laugh. 'When they start tryin' to kick the easy-dust habit after we're gone.'

Their voices trailed away along the passageway, and Jonmac sank back on to the ki-cloth, feeling shaken and sick. He wished desperately that there was something he could do. He had never felt a moment's anger or ill will towards the Stiks after the attack on the base, for he knew that the aliens had been tricked into it by the Dusters, as well as being half-crazed by easy-dust. Now, knowing that their sacred objects were to be ripped up and stolen, he felt only a deep and helpless sorrow.

Of course he had been sorrowing all along, since he had learned that he would be returned to Earth. He hated the fact that he would leave without seeing Rikil again, without having a chance to make a proper farewell between friends. He wished with all his heart that he could send a message to her – to warn her about the proposed theft of the statues, and to tell her he had always been her friend.

Those next few days were the worst of Jonmac's empty time in the cubicle. Daydreams gave way to waking nightmares as he imagined the Dusters' brutal response if any Stiks tried to defend their statues. With Rikil perhaps among them, facing the flamers . . .

Yet he was helpless, and hopeless, and trapped. He could do nothing but sit where he was, uselessly, and wait. Wait until the statues had been looted – wait for lift-off – wait for the final stages of Strake's plan, when the Dusters would probably get away with everything. Wait through more long and dismal hours that were interrupted only twice a day, morning and evening, when a Duster grumpily arrived with something for him to eat.

Three days later, however, even those interruptions stopped.

On that day, no one came with a morning meal. When Jonmac crept out to the washroom, no one could be heard nearby in the ship. After several more long, slow hours, he began to peer out into the passageway every few moments, to see if anyone was around. But no one was. So, when more time had passed, curiosity and suspicion and hunger finally overcame fear, and sent him out to prowl.

It was jumpy, tremulous prowling at first, where he was poised to turn and run if he heard a voice or a footstep. But the ship remained eerily silent. Growing bolder, he prowled on, through another passageway, then another. Meeting no one, hearing nothing.

They're probably just out trading, he thought, and someone forgot to feed me first. Or . . . maybe they're stealing the statues right now. Strake said they'd *all* go to do that.

He crept on, looking for the galley where he could find some food. But instead, by accident, he found himself in a broader passageway that led to the ship's airlock.

Staring at that solid barrier of metal, a crazy idea came into his mind. The idea of going *outside*.

The more he thought about it, the more he was sure he could do it. And the more he yearned to do it, if only for a moment. To breathe fresh cool air that held no foul smells – probably the last good air he'd breathe till they reached Earth. To take one last look at the forest of the Stiks.

He even thought for a foolish second that Rikil, somehow, by some coincidence, might be passing. Of course that was a silly notion . . . But still, he wanted to go out.

Not that he would try to *escape*, he thought. Where could he go? He was still desperately anxious to be returned to Earth, in that ship. But the idea of the breath of air, and of doing something that the Dusters had forbidden, appealed to him. And he was sure that he would hear and probably see the Dusters returning through the bush in plenty of time to get back into the ship unseen.

He peered at the airlock, braced against disappointment if after all he could not open it. But the manual controls were almost like those on the EXTRA ship. He fumbled at the switches – and at last, with a hiss that sounded disapproving, the airlock slid open. He stepped through it, out on to the narrow ramp, and took a deep breath of the moist air.

Then he nearly choked on it. Like tall, skeletal shadows, a group of about nine Stiks drifted noiselessly out of a thicket, almost in front of him.

Seeing him, the Stiks halted, speaking to one another in rustling whispers that sounded amazed. But they would be, he realized, if they *know who I am. They would have expected me to be gone with the* EXTRA *team. Maybe they think I've joined the Dusters . . .*

Slowly the Stiks moved closer, their spears half-raised. 'Onnak!' one of them suddenly said. He was the shortest of the group, and looked a bit like one of the young males from Rikil's family-group. Maybe she was nearby, Jonmac thought, and his heart leaped with sudden hope.

'Rikil come?' he asked, never wishing more fervently that he knew more of the alien language.

The shorter Stik said a quick word, with the 'no' gesture, which meant that Rikil was not there. Disappointed, Jonmac tried to think of something else to say, while starting to feel puzzled by the way the Stiks were holding their spears. As if *aimed* at him.

'Stikessi come trade?' he asked in their language. 'Cloth? *T'kii?*'

114

The spears seemed to twitch ominously. Then the shorter Stik spoke again, in his language, quite slowly as if making sure Jonmac would understand.

'We do not trade,' he said. 'Not for dust. We wish no trade, no dust. No more.'

Suddenly Jonmac felt afraid. A tendril of ice seemed to slide along his spine at the clear note of *finality* in the alien's voice. With a tone also of something very like a threat.

'No more *hikisti*!' one of the other Stiks echoed, raising his spear high. 'No more *enik-t'hikisti*!'

Jonmac stared, wondering if he understood correctly. The longer term seemed to mean 'ones-of-dust' – surely the Stik word for the Dusters.

'*Enik-t'hikisti*,' he repeated, trying to keep his voice from quavering. 'Where? Where they?'

The shorter Stik took a sudden stride forward, making Jonmac edge nervously back, up the ramp. 'They walked in the place of bare earth,' the Stik said. 'They went to tear up the *tistirrakai*.'

It was another word Jonmac had never heard. But he had no doubt it was the word for the statues in the clearing.

'Where . . . where are they?' Jonmac asked again, and that time the quaver did find its way into his voice.

'They are *k'nih'kli*,' the Stik said sharply, lifting his spear.

Again the word was new to Jonmac. But as the other Stiks shook their spears, repeating *k'nih'kli* like a chant, Jonmac's frightened gaze finally focused on the spear that was being held before his face. And the word's meaning became clear.

The sharp, oversized thorn that was the spear's head did not look polished and shiny as it should have. Nor did the spearheads of the others. Their gleam was covered by some kind of encrusting stain.

Recognizably, undeniably, the reddish-brown stain of dried blood.

12

While Jonmac's mind was just beginning to grasp the terrible truth, his body was taking him backwards up the ramp and into the ship in a panicky leap. His fingers jabbed wildly at the switches, and the airlock hissed shut to block his view of the Stiks holding up their gory spears like trophies. Sweaty and shaky, he sagged against the metal barrier, trying to stop his heart from leaping up into his throat.

Somehow, when the Dusters invaded the place of the statues, the Stiks had been able to fight them – and to defeat them. Perhaps by sheer weight of numbers, Jonmac thought. And he shuddered as he imagined how many of the aliens must have been blasted by the flamers' fire before the Dusters were overcome.

Yet the Stiks had won. The Dusters had paid the price for their intended desecration of the holy place. And then some of the aliens had come to the ship, to watch and wait and be sure no other Dusters lurked within.

But there aren't any others, Jonmac thought wildly. Only me.

Then the word 'only' forced its way past his panic and stabbed him more agonizingly than any spear.

He was alone.

He was the only human left on the planet.

He was marooned on an alien world.

And the beings of that world had just slaughtered six humans, having tried before at the EXTRA base to slaughter ten others.

He slid down the smooth metal of the airlock, dropping in a heap to the floor, wrapping his arms around him. Unknowingly he was making a hollow moaning sound, filled with despair – a hopeless empty crying of the soul, from the depths of his mind-twisting knowledge that he was alone on that planet. And not one other human being in the universe knew he was there.

Around him the Duster ship seemed to echo his cry, with the hollowness that is heard within a tomb. As the ship might well be, he knew, for him. He couldn't fly it, he didn't even know how to ignite its great engines. In time its stores of food and water would run out, or its life-support system would run down, or some electronic accident would wreck its circuits. And that would be the end of him.

His only alternative was to go back out – to face the spears of the vengeful Stiks. That would be the end of him, too.

Though at least, he thought in his anguish and despair, it would also be the end of his isolation, that immensity of aloneness.

For a long, unmeasured time he lay there by the airlock, curled into a ball – sometimes groaning aloud in his torment, sometimes weeping softly with eyes squeezed shut and every muscle clenched, sometimes lying motionless with eyes open and staring into nothing but the void of loneliness confronting him.

His horror and desolation was far greater than had been the case after the EXTRA team had left. Then, he had almost at once been given hope by the Dusters' decision to take him to Earth. But now, with the unimaginable breadth of half a galaxy between himself and his own world, his mind was reeling with a total, final abandoning of hope.

Under that onslaught, his mind tottered on the edge of a sort of oblivion. It might have left him mentally wrecked, a blank and shambling creature whose life would be even more shortened by insanity and helplessness.

But it did not happen. Wavering on that edge of madness, of total withdrawal from horror, his will still struggled instinctively to survive. And, because he had always been a healthy and well-balanced person, his will began to win that battle. His mind slowly drew back from that ghastly brink, while his body recognized how the battle had exhausted him, and slid away into the more healing oblivion of sleep.

When he woke, he was first aware of his aches and stiffness from sleeping on the hard floor. But as he heaved himself to a sitting position, staring around dull-eyed, remembrance surged over him like a shock wave of furious emotions. All the horror and pain and hopelessness came swarming back. *Alone*, his mind howled, and the word seemed to resonate mournfully like a funeral bell.

He felt his aloneness like an immense stifling weight descending upon him, crushingly, far beyond bearing. He fought to escape it, yet knew there was no escape. Scrabbling at the blank metal wall, he drew himself to his feet. And then he might have run through the ship in a mindless frenzy like a trapped beast, trying to leave the agony behind.

But he was distracted.

By a faint but definite *tapping*, on the airlock. From outside.

He stared with glazed eyes at the blank metal. The tapping sounded again, and he jerked, as if about to flee. But something perhaps born of his instinct to survive held him there.

It's those Stiks, he thought dazedly. Trying to get in, to use their spears on me. And for a quivering moment he was almost tempted to open the airlock and give himself to them, to put an end to his pain and horror.

But then his eyes widened as another possibility occurred to him. He lurched away, stumbling along the passages that led to the main control area – with its scanner systems, and their screens.

He had been shown how to work those switches, too. And when he had turned the scanners on, he looked at the screen showing the side of the ship where the airlock was. He stood looking for a long moment, swaying, staring at the image on the screen.

No Stiks with bloodied spears. No armed Stiks at all. Just one Stik who was empty-handed, save for a piece of hard bark that was being rapped steadily against the airlock. One small golden Stik, looking ready to stay there and knock on the ship for ever.

Rikil.

Jonmac hurried back to the airlock – but paused. What if Rikil was only enticing him out? What if the armed Stiks were waiting, hidden in the brush?

Once, he would have sworn that Rikil would

not betray him. At that moment, after all that had happened, he could not feel so sure.

At the same time, he was so desperately glad to see her – the one being on that planet who might in some way ease the suffering of his aloneness – that he was willing to risk it.

He reached for the switches, and the airlock slid open. He walked through it, stepped out on to the ramp, and looked into Rikil's enormous eyes.

'Onnak.' Her voice was breathy and shaky, and she was trembling in small spasms of emotion.

Jonmac glanced past her at the brush, saw no spearmen. 'Rikil,' he said, looking at her again. '*Nik'littin*. Welcome.'

'Other Stikessi said you are here,' she told him. Then she glanced warily up at the looming side of the Duster ship. 'Onnak is now *en t'hikisti*, one-of-dust?'

Jonmac stiffened. '*No!*' he replied, almost a shout. She flinched slightly, watching as he added the negative gesture. '*Enik t'hikisti . . .*' he began, but then he faltered. What were the alien words for capture, kidnap, imprisonment? He had no idea.

But she was waiting, her eyes almost pleading for an explanation. And somehow he found a way.

'Ones-of-dust *hold* me here,' he said, pronouncing the Stik words as carefully as he could. 'Not go. They not let me go. Hold.'

Slowly she blinked, delicate eyelids falling and rising like small curtains. 'I knew it was so,' she breathed. 'I told Stikessi that Onnak would not be one-of-dust.' She reached a wraith-like hand to rest it lightly on his arm. 'Your *il-lannari*,' she said. 'Your kin-group . . . Why did they leave you?'

The question, the sympathy in her voice and

touch, almost broke him down again. But he fought it, swallowing against the tightening of his throat. 'Did not know,' he said. 'Thought I was . . . *k'nih'kli*.'

Rikil's three-fingered grasp tightened on his arm. And then her sympathy wrecked his defences, and the storm of his emotions burst. He turned to lean his head against the ship's cool metal and wept, huge gasping sobs that seemed torn up from the centre of his being. Faintly, through the storm, he felt Rikil close beside him, her touch as soft as feathers, lightly stroking his back.

Her presence helped him to regain control, turning back to her at last, wiping his eyes on his sleeve. 'Sorry,' he gasped in his own language. 'It's . . . I just . . .'

Her hand rested on his arm again, light but reassuring. 'It is *inistik*,' she said, then saw him frown at the strange word. 'You have a thing you like,' she explained, 'then you do not have it. Gone. Lost. So there is *inistik*.'

'Yes,' Jonmac said, in his own language. 'Sadness. Grief.'

'Grief,' she repeated, then returned to the Stik tongue. 'All may feel grief when a thing is lost. But they must stop, in time. Too much grief, for too long a time, makes them turn from life. Makes them die.'

'Yes,' Jonmac whispered.

Her hand slid down his arm, took hold of his hand and gripped with amazing strength. 'Onnak will not die,' she said intensely.

He stared at her, feeling himself choke up again so that he could not have spoken even if he had known the words.

'Humans may come again,' she went on,

waving her other hand at the sky. 'Onnak must live, till they come.'

Jonmac stared up at the pale alien sky. An empty sky – and, he knew, likely to stay that way. There was very little chance that EXTRA would send another ship. They would know that there was nothing worth salvaging on the ruined base, and that the Dusters would be long gone, out of reach of punishment.

Above all, EXTRA's trade was finished on the planet. The team's departure would automatically revoke the EXTRA licence for that world. And since the team had left after a native uprising, there was little chance that a new licence would be issued. At least, not for a long time, perhaps years. Perhaps never.

And the chance of some other ship landing there was about the same as the chance of EXTRA returning in the near future. Almost none.

Still, he thought, if he could try not to think about that – try not to remember too much – try not to let himself feel that hopeless longing for Su and humankind and everything . . . Then he might just survive a while. Because Rikil was there.

Her presence, her concern, her determination to help him, had dragged him back from the edge. The terrible crushing enormity of his aloneness had been eased, a little. With Rikil, he could not be wholly alone.

Realizing that she was still watching him anxiously, he made the 'yes' gesture. 'I will live,' he told her, with a sigh.

Yet it was an immense promise. Glimpsing what it would mean, seeing a fragmentary vision of the kind of life and future he might face on that alien world, he grew suddenly weak, almost faint. He sagged down to slump heavily on to the ramp, Rikil joining him, still gripping his hand.

Don't think about it, he told himself fiercely. Don't think about the future or anything. Just get through this day, this hour, this minute. And then the next one . . .

He realized then that Rikil had spoken, a flurry of words that he hadn't listened to. At his puzzled look, she repeated the question.

'You will stay here?' Her gesture towards the ship seemed disapproving.

He made the 'no' gesture, wanting to tell her how horrible it was in the ship, how smelly and dirty and ugly. And how for him it would somehow contain the ghosts of the slaughtered Dusters. But he had no words for any of that. 'Not like,' he said at last, lamely.

She made an exaggerated 'yes' gesture, showing fervent agreement. 'Where will you be?'

'With you,' he blurted, the words emerging before his mind caught up with them.

Gently she squeezed his hand, then gestured 'no'. 'Onnak must live as a human,' she told him. 'Not with Stikessi. Stikessi need only the forest, the air and sky. Humans need *k'tilii*.'

Her free hand drew a shape in the air, and Jonmac understood. A house, a structure. Shelter. *K'tilii*.

Slowly he gestured 'yes'. And in that moment, though he had not given the question any thought at all till then, he knew exactly what he would do. Had to do.

'I will go back.' He pointed at the forest, in the general direction of the EXTRA base. 'To the place of my kin-group. I will be there.'

Rikil gazed at him serenely, her eyes bright.

'That is right. It is what must be. *Onnak's* place. And I will come there, often, to be with you. Day upon day. Many Stikessi will come.'

Jonmac felt suddenly chilled. Not since he had first come out of the ship to greet her had he thought again of the Stik spearmen, and the threat they had seemed to offer. Had he been wrong about that? Or was there a danger to him, from the adult Stiks, that Rikil did not know about?

He groped for the words, to form the questions. 'Other Stikessi . . .' he began.

But then he halted, his chill turning to iciness. Because it looked as if the question was going to be answered before it was asked.

In their usual eerie silence, a large group of Stiks – perhaps twenty or more – stepped out from the bush, spears and axes in hand, and advanced towards him.

13

Jonmac leaped up wildly, poised to flee into the ship and close the airlock against those spears. But Rikil clung to his hand, tugging him back.

'Wait!' she said. 'Stay!' And then she moved swiftly down the ramp to confront the Stiks.

Jonmac stared after her, shivering with fear and tension, on a ragged balance between wanting to run and wanting to know what she would do. And the Stiks came to a stop as Rikil faced them, some strides from the foot of the ramp. She was speaking to them urgently, almost crying out, her words pouring too fast for Jonmac to follow. And she seemed to be aiming her words especially at the tall Ilinit, leader of her own family group.

But all the Stiks crowded around to listen, sometimes looking up at Jonmac, their eyes dark and unreadable. Until at last Rikil's words came to an end, and Ilinit stepped away from the group to stare up the length of the ramp at Jonmac.

'Onnak.' His voice was quiet and calm. 'It is known now that the Stikessi did great wrong to your kin-group because of the *tistirraka* found at your place. It is known that the ones-of-dust tore up the *tistirraka*, as they tried later to tear up more *tistirrakai*.'

Jonmac shakily gestured 'yes'. 'It is so, Ilinit.'

'Some Stikessi,' Ilinit went on, 'thought Onnak had become one-of-dust. Now Rikil says it is not so. Is it not so, Onnak?'

Again Jonmac gestured, as expressively as he could. *'Not so.'*

The tall Stik looked at him intently, holding his gaze. It was a piercing look from the huge eyes, reminding Jonmac of the earlier, similarly searching gaze of Coln Robett, which had seemed to examine and weigh up the depths of his soul. Under that examination Jonmac was held motionless, hardly breathing, unable to think or speak.

Then at last Ilinit blinked, releasing the tension, and made a gesture unknown to Jonmac. 'It is not so. You are not one-of-dust.'

A stir, a ripple of movement and murmuring went through the other Stiks. A decision had been reached, a tension had been eased. And yet there was something else, for their eyes remained dark, and many of them began to tremble.

'The Stikessi have done your kin-group wrong,' Ilinit repeated. He was beginning to tremble as well. 'But they have done you, Onnak, most wrong of all. Your kin-group has been driven away into the sky. You are here, left alone, and Rikil says your kin-group does not know. To cause you to be alone is a great wrong. So . . . we must make *el'rillinel.'*

With slow dignity he stooped and placed his spear on the ground, stepping back from it. All the armed Stiks behind him did exactly the same, standing empty-handed, looking at Jonmac as if waiting. Jonmac, bewildered, turned to Rikil.

'El'rillinel,' she repeated. 'Onnak must say what it is to be. Take any thing, all things, that Stikessi have. *T'kii,* food, any thing. Or take Stikessi, any, all. *K'nih.'*

That last word sounded a bit familiar, but when Jonmac still looked bewildered Rikil pointed to a spear, then made a graphic mime of stabbing someone. '*K'nih*,' she repeated. 'Kill. Kill any, kill all. If Onnak says that is to be *el'rillinel.*'

Then, at last, Jonmac understood. The Stiks were offering him a way, probably a ritual way, to demand some kind of *penance* from them for the 'great wrong' they had done him. He could demand gifts, he could demand anything he liked. He could even, it seemed, demand their lives. *El'rillinel*, then, would mean – what was the word? – atonement.

And they seemed quite willing to stand there and let him kill, as many as he wished, until the debt was paid and the crime erased.

'I couldn't!' Jonmac gasped. 'I *can't*!' Then he made the most extravagant 'no' gesture he could manage, and said it as best he could in the Stik tongue. '*Not kill!*'

Again there was a ripple of sound through the unmoving Stiks, almost a buzz, and their trembling seemed to ease. As did Rikil's, while she looked towards him, her eyes brightening.

'I told the Stikessi you would not,' she said calmly. 'Your kin-group have not been like ones-of-dust. You have not hurt Stikessi, have not killed.'

'If Onnak will not kill,' Ilinit asked with equal calmness, 'what does he say must be *el'rillinel*?'

Jonmac looked at him helplessly, knowing that the ritual was important to the Stiks but having no idea what to do or say next. But as Rikil moved serenely towards him, her eyes even brighter, he was filled with a sudden inspiration. And a sure knowledge of what he really wanted, from the aliens.

Except he didn't know the word. 'What is it,'

he said confusedly to Rikil, 'that we have?' As she cocked her head on one side, not understanding, her eyes clouding a little, he tried again. 'Not *il-lannari*, kin-group, but like a kin-group. Like Rikil and Onnak.'

She blinked at him – and then her eyes cleared and she gestured happily. '*Narrira*,' she said softly, and her tiny hand moved up towards him, fluttering. 'Onnak and Rikil have *narrira*.'

Instinctively he repeated the movement, fluttering his hand towards her. At once she moved, stepping forward quickly, manoeuvring herself so that her fingertips touched his brow just as his touched hers.

'*Narrira*,' he echoed. 'Friendship.' He looked past her at the quietly watching Stiks. 'Onnak wants *narrira* with Stikessi.' Then, in another moment of inspiration, he added, '*narrira* is *el'rillinel*.'

From the group of Stiks arose a soft, rustling sigh, like a faraway breeze among branches. Then, in unison, as if perfectly choreographed, they all made the reaching, fluttering gesture of friendship towards Jonmac.

'*Narrira*,' they murmured, and sighed again as Jonmac returned the gesture with a trembling hand.

Then the Stiks stooped to reclaim their weapons, and drifted away into the forest without another word or sound. All except Rikil.

'When will you go,' she asked him softly, 'to your place? Your *k'tilii*?'

He would have said 'any time' if he had known the words. But then a realization struck him. When he had been captured, Wace had thrown all his belongings into the fire. Including the little responder, that would have guided him home. If the transmitter on the base had survived, which was unlikely.

'I . . . I don't know the way,' he said unhappily.

She took a moment to understand, then laughed her soft, humming laughter. 'Rikil will show you,' she said.

He gazed at her with new gratitude, almost overwhelmed as he saw the total immensity of his debt to her, then and in the future. And then, despite all the pain and loss and desolation he had been suffering, despite that whole terrible roller-coaster of emotion, some irrepressible part of his mind came up with a remark that was an absurd, ironic joke. A silly thing that one small child might say to another. Except that in his case it was poignantly, literally true.

'Oh, Rikil,' he said in his own language, 'you're my best friend in the whole world!'

Then he burst out laughing, wild laughter bubbling up and overflowing. Not quite spilling over into hysteria, but near enough to make him sag weakly back against the ship, half-collapsing as he laughed. And Rikil laughed with him, not understanding but infected by his laughter. Until at last they had to sit down on the ramp, limp and weak and gasping as their laughter faded and calmed and died away.

They sat there for several quiet moments, leaning against each other. And Jonmac felt willing to stay there indefinitely, amazed at how much better he felt not only because she was there but because of the healing release of the laughter.

After a while, they rose quietly together and walked away into the forest. And Jonmac did not once look back at the Duster ship as he set off with his friend towards the place where he would live.

Stepping back on to the EXTRA base, or what was left of it, almost plunged Jonmac back into the depths of horror and despair. It was all so familiar . . . and yet his mother was not there to scold him for being away so long, the starship was not there, and nearly every other sign of a human presence was shattered and destroyed.

As if sensing the anguish of his reaction, Rikil took his hand again, trying to comfort him, trying also to divert him. 'Where will you be?' she asked softly. 'Where will you have *k'tilii?*'

The simple practicality of the question dragged Jonmac back from the abyss. Taking a deep breath, he looked around, trying to see the ruins as presenting problems to be solved, not reminders of grief and loss.

The outer buildings of the base, most vulnerable to the Dusters' flamers, simply no longer existed. Including the one where he had been hiding when the attack began. The plastishell fabric of the buildings had burned with immense ferocity, so that nothing remained except what looked like pools of hardened tar, mingled with ash and charred fragments from whatever had been inside the buildings.

That's what Su probably thinks I am now, he thought morbidly. Ashes and burnt bits. But with an effort he pushed the grisly thought away, forcing himself to think usefully.

At the far end of the base, closest to where the starship had been, two of the small buildings had partly survived. One had considerable fire damage to its roof, the other was missing most of two walls. But one or the other would do, he thought. Better than trying to sleep under a bush in the rain.

'There,' he said to Rikil, pointing. *'K'tilii.'*

When he went to look at the semi-intact buildings Rikil hung back, with the usual Stik reluctance to enter a human enclosure. But she came to peer anxiously through the doorway of the roofless building when Jonmac, inside, gave a muffled cry of delight.

Wace had said that some things had survived or had been left behind, including food, and Jonmac found that the Duster had not exaggerated. The roofless building contained the mess hall, the team's eating place, where against a rear wall Jonmac found several large insul-crates of food, with scarcely a scorchmark. He also remembered that the Duster ship held a supply of the basic protein concentrate. So he wouldn't go hungry, not for a long time.

Best of all, he found in the mess hall – also nearly untouched by flames – a tall console that had been one of the base's most crucial pieces of technology. The water recycler. Anxiously he touched its controls, and gave another half-cheer as it throbbed briefly and produced a stream of clear water. He sipped, grinned and switched it off. The recycler had its own power-source, and seemed in perfect condition.

Of course there was water in the Duster ship's life-support, too. But he decided he would keep it all for drinking. He could wash in a forest pool when necessary. And he was even able to manage a painful half-smile as he thought of what his mother would have said about that.

There was little else, though, in the roofless

building and nothing at all in the other building, the one lacking two walls, except a damaged table and some fragments of charred clothing. But there was at least a small room in one corner whose walls had survived, away from the open side of the building. That, he thought, would be his bedroom, his lair. And he could raid the Dusters' store of ki-cloth for his bedding – as much as I want, he thought, thinking of the ship's crammed cargo holds.

He felt some disappointment, since he had been hoping, irrationally, that some intact equipment might have been left behind. Of course, much of it had been powered from the starship, but he had been wishing for one of the portable, self-powered vid-screens and some tapes. Or even some of the little music-beads that could be worn in the ear. But nothing like that remained in either building. On the other hand, there were also no personal computers or terminals containing the software for his schoolwork. And that made him think wrenchingly of his mother again.

He controlled his thoughts, trying to organize himself. Lots to do, he thought. Trips to the Duster ship to bring back ki-cloth and food and things. He'd have to mark a trail, in case Rikil wasn't there to guide him. He didn't look forward to going back into the ship, with its echoing, tomb-like silence. But it had to be done.

Just as he would have to comb through every centimetre of the ash and burnt plastic, over all the base, in case other useful intact items lay hidden beneath the destruction. And he would need to find a way to cover the shattered windows and ruined walls of the second building, to keep rain and weather away from his lair. Lots to do . . .

But he was thinking about all that work with some *relief*, more than anything, as he went out to rejoin the patiently waiting Rikil. Having things to keep him busy, he knew, was a sure way to keep his pain, his desolation, from overwhelming him.

It won't be so bad, he told himself determinedly. He had the basics, food and water and shelter. He had the unexpected gift of friendship from the Stiks. And he had the measureless comfort and companionship of his one special friend.

There were other things, a galaxy of things, that he might have wished for. But he would not let himself make wishes. His courage, his resilience, and the brightness in Rikil's eyes as he went to join her, reminded him that he might have had far *less*.

In that moment he tried as hard as he could to feel *glad* of what few things he had. And tried in the same way, with all the inner resources he could muster, to make himself ready to face whatever future lay before him, on that world.

14

He expected his first night back on the base to be nearly unbearable. Remarkably, he was wrong.

When the afternoon shadows began to lengthen, Rikil had to leave to find her kin-group. Jonmac wanted to beg her to stay but knew better than to try. He walked with her a short way into the forest, turning back before the base was out of sight. Alone again, entering the building where his chosen bedroom was, he automatically reached for the pressure pad to turn on the lights.

Nothing happened, and he grimaced with disgust. No power without the starship, he thought. Except for the self-powered water recycler. So no lights. Good thing I don't need heat here, he thought grimly, trying to be calm about it. I'll just get up at dawn, go to bed at nightfall, like the birds. Or like the *bugs*, he amended, thinking of the forest's wildlife. Probably like the Stiks, too.

In the deepening twilight he went to the mess hall and opened one of the crates of food, taking out a small thermafoil container. Pulling the tab, he waited for the foil to heat the contents, then opened it. It turned out to be an all-purpose stew, one of his favourite things on the base's limited menu.

He took that as a good omen, needing all the good ones he could get. After eating, with darkness descending, he gathered all the fragments of charred clothing, rolling and bunching them into a poor imitation of a pillow. Then he stretched out on the floor in his little room, pillow under his head, thinking longingly of soft heaps of ki-cloth.

Even so, amazingly, as warm food and weariness took effect on him, he found himself feeling relaxed and sleepy. And in the midst of that good feeling he allowed himself – very tentatively, experimentally – to look at that part of his mind where all the emotions of grief and loneliness and despair were still massed and waiting.

It was like opening the door of a haunted house, when he *knew* that beyond it lurked a host of horrors eager to leap out and drag him down. After the briefest possible glimpse of the waiting horrors he slammed the door again, forcing himself to think of other things, to turn his mind back to calmness.

Tomorrow, he thought. Think about tomorrow. If Rikil comes, she can take me back to the Duster ship. Don't forget to mark a trail. And I can search the ship. What if *they* have a vid-screen? And he ordered his thoughts on to that subject, thinking about what tapes the Dusters might have, what ones he would like them to have . . .

In the midst of such comparatively pain-free thinking, he quite effortlessly fell asleep.

He was a little surprised to have slept, when he awoke in the grey light of early morning. Surprised, too, that he felt refreshed despite some stiffness from sleeping on the floor. And he felt even better after a good breakfast from another container out of the food crate.

Now and then he probed, ever so delicately, at the part of his mind where his most painful feelings were held, the lurking horrors. Of course they were still there. But he found that he could manage more securely to keep his guard up against them.

It was like walking a fine line, a razor-edge of peace between tormenting memories of the past and unnerving worries about the future. Not to mention all the other destructive thoughts, of might-have-been and if-only . . . It was the hardest thing he had ever had to do, keeping his balance on that fine line. Nonetheless, he balanced.

Instinct told him that his best protection from the horrors was to concentrate without wavering on the idea of *one day at a time.* While being sure to make each of those days as *full* as possible, to keep his mind occupied.

So having lots to do would be a blessing. Having Rikil there would be a great blessing. And in the course of that morning, as he clung to his blessings, he began to enter the first shaky stages of *acceptance.* Accepting reality, accepting that things were as they were and could not be changed by grieving. It was as essential to his survival as food and water, and more essential than anything else.

In fact he seemed almost serene when Rikil arrived halfway through the morning. He had begun to sift through the remains of another building, to see if anything had survived. But he readily left that work and went, with Rikil as guide again, back to the Duster ship. She laughed a little as he made sure to mark the path, with bent branches and twisted twigs. And he was able to laugh with her, which made him almost cheerful as they reached the ship.

He had left the airlock open, the day before, which had improved the smell a little inside. And the support system was still working, of course, so there was light enough to banish spooki-ness. Though he knew that he would never be able to stay on the ship after dusk began to fall.

Still, that day and the next few days, the daylight hours allowed him to make a thorough search of the vessel. But he found very little, in the men's quarters, of any use. Just their lurid, tattered clothes and assorted junk. Sadly, there were no vid-screens, no portable computers, no music beads. The only form of 'entertainment' he found was a collection of small, revoltingly pornographic holo-images.

Nor were there any weapons on the ship. Clearly the Dusters carried all their weaponry with them. So the flamers and everything would still be with the bodies, probably sunk in some forest bog.

Grimacing at that idea, he went at last to search the ship's galley. As expected, the food stores were mainly a stack of heavy crates full of the protein concentrate. With the food from the EXTRA base, he reckoned he had enough to eat for a year.

He refused to think about what he would do then. One day at a time, he reminded himself firmly.

When the searching was done, he began dragging the crates of food to the airlock, one at a time, ready to be taken back to the base. It would be no fun, he knew, struggling with them through the bush. Each one would take hours of slow, backbreaking toil.

'Never mind, Onnak,' he said aloud, using his Stik name in self-mockery. 'There's no rush. You have all the time in the world.'

He also took large quantities of ki-cloth to the airlock, to be taken to the base. And finally, when everything else was done, he collected up all the Dusters' personal possessions, including the holo-porn, and heaped it up in the galley. Then he added to the heap the one important thing the Dusters had owned.

A quantity of large, bulging pouches containing the remaining supplies of easy-dust.

Jonmac had never tried the dust. He had thought, earlier, that he would find it – and he knew that it would allow him to spend much of his foreseeable future in a pleasurable daze, untroubled by the horrors of grief and despair. It was a powerful temptation.

But what, he wondered, would it do to his mind? What would happen when it ran out? What if there was an emergency when he needed to be alert, not dazed? He recalled what he had seen on the day he had first discovered the Dusters. The addicted Stiks, lurching and staggering, clownish and absurd, robbed of all their stately silent dignity.

That's what the dust does, he thought. And it made the Stiks attack the base. The dust is part of an ugly kind of life, like the Dusters lived. Not me.

Grimly he began to pick up the pouches, and all the other heaped clutter, feeding it all slowly into the mouth of the ship's disposal unit. Behind its shielding the unit clicked on, with a faint grinding noise. The ferocity of its energies, he knew, would incinerate anything, leaving almost no residue.

'That's it, now, Onnak,' he muttered to himself. 'There's no vid, no music, no dust, nothing. If you're going to make it, you have to make it on your own.'

But I *will* make it, he thought fiercely, as if in

reply. I have everything I need for survival. So I'll survive.

One day at a time.

When he began taking the salvaged goods back to the base, he chose to start with a relatively easy load of ki-cloth. Halfway along his marked path, Rikil found him, saw what he was doing, made a gesture that said 'wait', and vanished. Shortly she returned with several members of her kin-group including the leader, the 'group-father', Ilinit.

The Stiks' spindly limbs were uncannily strong, and made short work of the transfer of goods. Even the big, awkward insul-crates of food were whisked from ship to base with no great effort. Jonmac had to drag the things out of the ship and stow them away on the base by himself, for the Stiks would not enter any structure. But the labour that might have taken him weeks, if he could have managed the crates at all, took the Stiks only a few days.

When he tried to express his thanks, Ilinit made a kindly gesture. 'We are pleased to help you, Onnak. This, too, is *el'rillinel*.'

Jonmac was startled to realize that the Stiks were still concerned about atonement. He was further startled, in the time that followed, when other Stiks as well as Rikil and her kin-group began to visit him, with gifts, more offerings of *el'rillinel*.

They brought him small ornaments and arte-facts, necklaces or armlets of wooden beads, tiny carvings of polished wood. They brought offerings of food, produce of the forest, especially things like large nuts that were mealy and sweet. Jonmac was less pleased when they brought fresh kills from a hunt – some of the larger insectile creatures, often with legs or wings still twitching. He accepted them politely, then quietly buried them after the Stiks were gone.

Once Ilinit himself gave Jonmac a special gift – a Stik spear, with its long thorn spearhead. So he might hunt for himself, the group-father said. Jonmac felt no more inclined to hunt bugs than to eat them, but he was delighted with the spear. And though other Stiks sometimes gave him weapons, Ilinit's spear remained his favourite.

In between visits from Stiks, he worked. He cleared away all the charred and melted remnants of the base, then fastened ki-cloth over the buildings, like curtains, where the roof and walls had been. He did all those labours and other routine chores slowly and carefully, letting them fill his time and his thoughts until the next enjoyable interruption by Rikil or other visiting Stiks.

But some interruptions were more disturbing. Then his visitors were Stiks with torn and fouled robes, trembling like saplings in a wind, unable to keep their balance, yet carrying huge bundles of ki-cloth. They would drop the cloth at Jonmac's feet and cry out pleadingly.

'*Hikisti!*' they would beg. '*Hikisti!*'

'No *hikisti*,' Jonmac would tell them. 'No dust. All gone.'

Then the addicted Stiks would howl, a terrible desperate sound, and lurch off into the bush, leaving Jonmac appalled and saddened. As he was when Rikil told him of the addicts' suffering, many of them dying, others half-crippled in mind or body. And he would think that the Dusters had deserved their fate. For bringing that pollution to the Stiks, he thought, the Dusters had made their own savage *el'rillinel*.

Sometimes during those days and weeks, for a change, Jonmac would leave his work on the base and wander in the bush nearby – exploring, making himself familiar with that part of the forest. Only rarely did he fail to find something of interest: more of the alien creatures, oddly shaped trees or plants, dark forest pools. As he roamed, ranging farther from the base, marking his trails, he grew more and more comforted by the peace of 'his' forest, where he had nothing to fear except the risk – becoming less every day – of getting lost.

Or so he thought. Until a day when he was struggling up a steep slope, tangled with undergrowth, more than two hours' walk from the base. As he climbed, a creature burst out of hiding almost at his feet. It was thin and hairy, the size of a rat, with powerful hind legs made for jumping. As it leaped into the air, terrified, it narrowly missed Jonmac's face. He jerked back by reflex, with one foot tangling in some knotted roots. Overbalancing, he fell backwards down the slope – and as his foot twisted free, he cried out with the sudden explosion of agony in his ankle.

He tumbled to the foot of the slope, lashed and scratched by twigs but feeling nothing except the pain in his ankle. And then, as he lay there, with the pain came terror.

With that much pain, the ankle had to be broken. And he was in the depths of the forest, in an overgrown gully, a very long way from the base. Alone and unable to walk. With no supplies or equipment of any sort.

The terror swept over him, blotting out the pain.

He saw with fearful clarity how careless he had been for so long, and how lucky. He had never thought about the chance of having an accident, or perhaps falling ill. And now it had happened, and he was helpless. Even if Rikil and the Stiks came looking for him, they might never find him there in that plant-choked gully. Or might not find him in time.

He had been totally, horribly *vulnerable*, all along. And now he was totally alone, and injured. He had thought he was doing a great job of surviving, in the alien forest. But he could *die*, right there in that gully.

Panic rose within him, and he moaned, flinching away from his own fear. The movement stirred up more of the white-hot pain in his ankle, and he moaned again, struggling to sit up, to look at the injury. The ankle was swelling fast, puffing over the top of his low boot. Automatically he reached down to unfasten the boot, hoping to ease the pain a little. And somehow that action, trying to do something to help himself, also pushed away some of the fear and panic.

This is stupid, he told himself shakily. I'm not dying. I'm not helpless. I can move. And so – I'd better start.

Clenching his jaw, he forced himself to wriggle slowly towards the nearest clump of trees, grunting with the electric jolts of agony in his ankle. With some effort he managed to break off a sapling, and with its help dragged himself upright. Using it as a crutch, he moved away in a clumsy, hopping lurch.

Time moved as slowly and painfully as he did. The damaged ankle shrieked with every jerk and hop, but he went grimly on. Sometimes he sobbed, sometimes he swore, mostly he just breathed hard through gritted teeth. Now and then he missed his step and fell, lying still awhile, squeezing his eyes shut against tears of pain, gasping for breath. But then he would struggle up again, and hobble on.

Through all that, another fear – of being lost – kept him just as grimly focused on his marked trail. Until at last, after what had felt like a lifetime, exhausted and sweat-drenched and agonized, he lurched out of the forest on to the base, and home.

In his lair he wrapped the swollen ankle in ki-cloth that he had soaked in cool water. Then he simply collapsed on his bed, not knowing what else to do – having no idea how to set a broken ankle, having none of the swift-healing medications that he had once taken for granted. Eventually, as weariness overcame pain, he fell into a restless sleep, to dream of endless one-legged struggles through an unforgiving forest.

When he woke, it was early morning – and Rikil was there, looking anxiously in from outside the building. The wrapping had come away from the ankle, which looked like a fiery red balloon, not seeming to belong to a human leg. And Rikil trembled with distress and sympathy as Jonmac dragged himself outside to tell her what had happened.

'Onnak is *ilii-ra*,' she said, 'to come through the forest like that.'

Jonmac had the idea that the word meant something like 'tough' or 'hardy', but he lacked the energy to ask, or to feel pride at the compliment. In any case, Rikil was moving away.

'I will bring *hirelri*,' she told him. And then she

was gone, leaving Jonmac trying to work out what she could have meant.

In the next while he also tried to avoid looking at his ankle, wondering if Rikil could help in any way, wondering if he would be permanently crippled. But shortly the first of those questions was answered, when Rikil returned with an armful of soft, flaky bark – *hirelri*.

Crushing some of the bark, she mixed it with water and soft soil to make a dark, muddy paste, which she gently smeared on the damaged ankle before wrapping it again in wet ki-cloth. The coolness was blissful on the tormented swelling – and it continued, for Rikil stayed with Jonmac all day, often renewing the poultice. By evening, when she had to leave, the ankle's agony was noticeably less fierce, so that night Jonmac slept more peacefully.

Next morning, he discovered two remarkable things. First, amazingly, the swelling was much smaller. And when he nervously, flinchingly tested the ankle, he found that he could move it. The pain was ferocious – but it moved. It wasn't broken.

Just a bad sprain, he guessed. And so it proved, over the next few days, as it got better with astonishing speed thanks to more applications by Rikil of the healing bark. It all made Jonmac feel a little shamefaced, remembering how he had lain in the gully fearing that he would die there, when he only had a sprained ankle.

And yet that fear had not been just a joke, a silliness. The realization that had come to him then still held true. He *had* been lucky, so far, because he *was* vulnerable – to accident, injury, disease. He could no longer ever allow himself to be careless or unwary, especially in the forest. Because another time, another mischance, might *well* be the end of him.

Even so, as he often thought during those days of healing, he had been wrong about part of the fear that had overcome him in the gully. He was not alone. He could count on the Stiks, or at least on Rikil. The accident seemed to have shown her, too, just how vulnerable Jonmac was. From then on she came to the base to see him every day, without fail. And their friendship blossomed even more rapidly, through all those days.

Like any two young people growing more at ease with one another, they talked together, non-stop, almost all the time. And because Jonmac was talking only with her and other Stiks, his knack for languages was rapidly, almost effortlessly, making him fluent in the Stik tongue. The more fluent he became, the more easily he and Rikil talked – about everything and anything – and the more their closeness developed.

Later, when his ankle was fully healed, they took to rambling in the forest together while they talked. And for Jonmac, those rambles were educational without giving him any feeling of being taught. Rikil might describe in detail some part of her kin-group's nomadic life, or inform him about the different plants and animals they saw along the way. She was amused when he began carrying Ilinit's spear with him, and also when he tried clumsily to move in the bush with a Stik's easy silence. But steadily, over that time, he improved. He learned the ways of the forest from Rikil just as he learned the language.

One day, for fun, she wrapped a length of ki-cloth around him like a Stik garment, folding and draping it, twisting and tucking it. Then she looked at him with a soft hum of laughter.

'Onnak is becoming Stikessi,' she announced.

He felt absurdly pleased at the words. And when he had learned to wrap the cloth for himself, he wore it often, instead of his own clothes – though he kept his boots. Soon Rikil no longer laughed but simply accepted it as natural. Just as she accepted that he usually carried the spear, and that sometimes he could slip through a thicket with her without disturbing a leggy bug-thing only a few paces away.

But never, in all those days of wandering and talking together, did Rikil ever refer to one special detail of her people's life – the forbidden clearing with the weirdly beautiful statues. The *tistirrakai*, as they were called.

By then Jonmac knew that the word meant something like 'earth-dreamers'. And he was still deeply curious about the objects. But he knew that he had to wait until Rikil raised that delicate subject – which she never did.

Still, despite that blank spot, he knew that he was acquiring more insight into the life of an alien race than any scientist could ever achieve from the outside. And perhaps the most important insight, as he later understood, grew out of a time when he was idly telling Rikil about a trip he and his mother had once taken, on Earth, to see the last few remaining acres of the Amazon rain forest.

'You wouldn't believe those trees, Rikil,' he said dreamily. 'I wish I could take you to Earth and show you.'

To his surprise she began laughing, as if he had made the funniest joke in the galaxy. And when she was finally able to explain, he still couldn't see the joke.

Apparently, for Rikil, the idea of leaving her world was so unthinkable as to be hilarious.

'I could not leave, Onnak,' she told him. 'I am Stikessi, and the place of Stikessi is *here*.'

'But I left my world,' Jonmac protested. 'You could leave yours, if there was a ship . . .'

Her 'no' gesture was emphatic. 'Humans go everywhere through the sky, as you have told me. Perhaps that is because they do not have a place that is *their* place, their ground. But Stikessi do. We have this ground.' She tapped a foot lightly on the soil for emphasis. 'We come from this ground and return to it. We are a part of the ground, just as the trees are, and the ground is part of us. Do you see, Onnak? The forest, the ground, the Stikessi . . . all are part of one thing. The forest cannot fly away from the ground, the ground cannot walk away from the forest. Nor can Stikessi.'

'But . . .' Jonmac began. Then, wisely, he stopped.

There was a resonance in her words that seemed almost religious. And his EXTRA training made him respectful of alien religions. His feelings for Rikil made him even more so.

Maybe that's why the Stiks are the way they are, he thought. So silent and calm and peaceful. Because they have a special bond to their land, their world.

The thought returned to him later, when he was alone that night. And with it came sad thoughts of how far he was from his own world, from people with whom he had a bond. For the first time in some while, that night, he had to struggle violently against a new attack of what he called the horrors, as grief and loss and desolation swept over him once again.

He won that struggle, as he had won the others before it. But as he finally fell into a fitful sleep his face was wet with tears and his dreams were tortured nightmares.

Nearly a week later, nightmare also came by day.

15

In the intervening days, Rikil had been to the base only once. And she had seemed tired and agitated, and had stayed only briefly. Jonmac had felt perturbed, worrying that he had upset her somehow.

When she finally returned after some days, he was nearly sure of it. Her great eyes were darkened, and her golden-furred body was trembling in the grip of some powerful emotion.

'Onnak,' she said rapidly before he could even greet her. 'I am here to s-say . . . f-farewell. I c-can come no m-more. I d-do not know if I w-will see you again.' The stutter underlined her distress.

He gaped at her, horrified. *'Why?'* he almost shouted. 'What is it? What have I done?'

Her 'no' gesture was like a spasm. 'It is not . . . You have d-done nothing. It is m-my . . . my *time*. To depart.'

'But why?' Jonmac repeated desperately. 'Can't you tell me?'

She was backing away, her body vibrating. 'It is what m-must be, Onnak. I c-can say . . . no more. I m-must go.' She paused for an instant, blinking rapidly. 'We have been l-like *il-lannari*, a kin-group, you and I. D-do not forget m-me, Onn-nak . . .'

'Rikil!' Jonmac cried. But the forest swallowed her up, and his cry went unanswered.

That night the horrors swarmed back into his mind, and he found few defences against them.

He lay awake, staring blindly into the darkness, sometimes racked by dry sobs. He could not think, however he tried, what he might have done to drive her away. Yet he blamed himself, agonizing over her loss.

And with that came his other agonies, his other losses and lonelinesses. He groaned and writhed on his anguished bed, sometimes crying out help-lessly into the indifferent night. Until finally, with emotions ravaged and drained, he fell into an exhausted sleep. But daylight came seemingly at once, to rouse him to further torment. He staggered up, unable to think of anything to do, any real reason to go on with anything at all, there on his own, without Rikil . . .

Then he saw the Stik, standing motionless at the forest's edge.

It was Ilinit, Rikil's group-father, regarding Jonmac with dark unreadable eyes. I *have* offended Rikil somehow, Jonmac thought emptily. Maybe he wants atonement from *me* now.

'Ilinit,' he croaked in greeting.

'Onnak.' The tall Stik made a gesture that Jonmac did not know, but that did not seem unfriendly. 'Rikil comes no more.'

Jonmac gestured 'yes' jerkily. 'She did not say why. If I have offended, I will offer *el'rillinel*.'

The Stik twitched as if startled. 'There has been no offence, Onnak. She did not tell you because she thought it would not be permitted.' He paused as if gathering his thoughts. 'You have become Rikil's friend and our friend, Onnak. You speak our words, you eat our food. So in the *il-lannari* it has been decided. Though you are not Stikessi, you may be permitted to know.'

'Know what?' Jonmac asked, tensing against new shock.

'Why Rikil comes no more,' Ilinit said quietly. 'It is her time, Onnak. Her time to leave us all. Her time to return to the ground, from which we all first came.'

She's going to *die*, Jonmac thought in terror. He felt his legs were going to give way, as the paralysis of panic came over him. But he tried to fight free, tried to make his mouth work. 'What . . . what do you mean?' he gasped.

Again Ilinit made a gesture he did not know. 'It is her time,' he repeated. 'To set this life aside and rejoin the ground, which is the Source and Renewal of all things. It is a time that must come to all Stikessi.'

Everything around Jonmac seemed to be collapsing into fragments. She *can't* die, he cried within himself. Why should she? What's wrong with her? How could it be? But at the same time he was remembering Rikil's strange, troubled farewell, the day before. And he knew then just what kind of goodbye she had been making.

'For Stikessi,' Ilinit was calmly continuing, 'the rejoining is a private and special time, a holy thing. Only *il-lannari*, the kin-group, are there to help and watch. But Rikil has asked that *you* be there, Onnak. She says that you and she are a sort of *il-lannari*. So we have spoken of this matter, and have decided. You may be there.'

Jonmac stared, knowing that it was an immense honour to be invited to a sacred and private alien rite. But it was an honour he wanted to refuse, an event he didn't want to happen. I *can't*, he wailed within himself. Go and watch Rikil die?

Then come back here alone, to be alone the rest of my life?

He had no relationship with any other Stik as he had with Rikil. None of the closeness where they could understand each other so well across the barrier of their alienness. I don't *want* her to die, he shrieked within his mind, I don't *want* her to leave me . . .

No doubt his expression and stance showed something of his inner torment, for Ilinit took a step towards him, his voice sounding sympathetic. 'It is not a time to be sad, Onnak. The rejoining is a welcome thing. Though she must leave us, we do not grieve. We accept it gladly, because it is what must be.'

The quiet fatalism of those words did little to ease Jonmac's pain. But they did help him to regain some control over himself, so as not to fall apart in front of Ilinit. And the alien, seeing that, made a small gesture of approval.

'You will be there, Onnak?' he asked gently.

Jonmac looked away, hearing his inner voice still crying out, I don't *want* to . . . 'When is it?' he asked, his voice creaking.

Ilinit gestured up towards the sun that was climbing through broken cloud. '*S'kihir*. In one day. When the morning is advanced almost to the centre of the day.'

Jonmac quivered, then fought to regain stillness. 'What . . . what would I have to do?'

'Nothing, Onnak,' Ilinit said softly. 'There is nothing for anyone to do, except Rikil. We others can only be with her, to wait with her and support her, till it is done. I will come for you, Onnak. Soon after the sun's return, *s'kihir*.'

He made the fluttering gesture of friendship,

153

which Jonmac shakily returned, and silently slipped away into the bush.

Alone then, and knowing the totality and permanence of that aloneness, Jonmac sank slowly to his knees. His upper body drooped slowly forward until his head was nearly touching the ground, to make himself as small and tightly crumpled a ball as possible. And all the re-awakened horrors of grief and loss and hopelessness came thundering down upon him like an avalanche.

He wanted to stay like that for ever. He wanted to find a way for himself to 'rejoin the ground', or anyway find some release from pain. But before long his healthy body dragged him back to an awareness of other things, including his cramped position. At last he rose and stumbled back to his small bleak room.

For the rest of that day his mind presented, unstoppably, an endless series of images of Rikil, like vid-tapes for his private viewing. All the treasured moments were there, all the closeness and warmth of the past weeks. He saw her again as she was when they had first seen each other and tentatively, nervously approached each other. He saw her again as she was on that last day when she had said she must go, without saying what kind of fateful going she meant.

Reliving those memories, Jonmac knew that he loved Rikil. Also, with a flash of mature wisdom, he knew that it was a strange sort of love, between a human and an alien, which would no doubt have led to *some* sort of sad farewell in the end.

He could never have foreseen that they would be parted by her premature death. But if he had flown away from her world as he had expected to do, with the EXTRA team or with the Dusters, it would have been just as permanent and painful a goodbye.

That made his pain no less, but it began to make it more bearable, more acceptable. He thought of her words, as she left him, entreating him not to forget her. And he recalled some other words that he had once heard on the vid. 'No one is ever dead,' someone had said, 'as long as there are those who keep remembering them.'

So you won't die, Rikil, he promised her silently. Because I won't forget you.

He gritted his teeth and shook his head to fight off tears. He would have to do that quite often the next day, he thought, when Ilinit took him to watch Rikil die. I don't *want* to, he cried silently once again. But he knew he would go.

Not because it was a unique honour for a human to be included in a sacred alien ceremony. Simply because Rikil wanted him there.

I'll be there, his inner voice promised her. Whatever you want of me . . . I won't let you down.

Without being aware of what he was doing, he slowly moved his hand in a sketchy version of the Stiks' friendship gesture.

And the next morning he was waiting – wrapped in his ki-cloth, dry-eyed and resolute – when Ilinit came to collect him.

The group-father said little, merely peering intently at Jonmac before turning and leading the way into the bush. As he followed, Jonmac felt a strange numbness creeping over his emotions, as if they wanted a lull in that time of torment. Also, it seemed important that he should move through

155

the bush as quietly as he could behind the almost noiseless Ilinit, as if unnecessary sound would show disrespect to Rikil and her passing.

So intent was he on moving with silence that he hardly noticed their route, or how far they were travelling. But it seemed to have been more than an hour when they came suddenly upon Ilinit's kin-group, waiting beside a thicket as if expecting them. The thicket, its branches bent and woven into a temporary roof, had clearly been the group's sleeping-place the previous night, or perhaps more than one night.

At its heart, to which Ilinit and the others led Jonmac, lay Rikil.

She was lying on something like a stretcher, two long poles joined by a lattice of woven branches. Instead of her usual short garment she was covered by an enormous wrapping of ki-cloth, swathed around and around her in voluminous folds from her neck to her feet, leaving only her head exposed. She looked tiny and helpless, lying there, and somehow shrunken. And Jonmac saw with a jolt that she had lost most of the soft golden fur that had covered her head.

As her gaze turned slowly towards him, her eyes looked even huger in her wizened face, with shadowy colours in their depths that he had never seen before.

It took every scrap of courage and character that Jonmac could find to keep him from falling to his knees again and howling. But Rikil's shadowed eyes seemed to grip him, to hold him still. Motionless, he stared back at her, hearing Ilinit's voice as if from a long way away.

'They have begun,' Ilinit was saying quietly. 'The changes, that signal the time of rejoining.

Rikil cannot speak now, and her body grows still. But she may still be able to hear you, Onnak, if you would speak to her.'

He didn't think he could speak. His mouth felt numb and his throat felt as if he was being strangled. But she deserved more than that, he told himself fiercely. And somehow he forced out the words past the choking grip of grief. The same words that he had vowed silently the night before.

'I will never forget you, Rikil,' he told her. 'Never while I live.'

Something flickered deep in her darkened eyes, as if to tell him that she had heard. But then Ilinit was motioning him back, as four of the other Stiks picked up the stretcher, lifting it as if Rikil was weightless.

As they all moved away through the bush, Jonmac trailed along behind Ilinit, half-drowning in his grief. The Stiks seemed no less calm and silent than ever, moving fairly quickly, glancing up at the sky now and then. When the sun burst forth through broken cloud, they all murmured something, words unknown to Jonmac. And Ilinit explained, with a strange gladness in his voice.

'The sun will put its light on her rejoining,' he said. 'It is a great blessing.'

Jonmac nodded, feeling too numb to speak, feeling that nothing about Rikil's passing could be seen as a blessing. Even so, something at the back of his mind was slowly becoming aware that he had been in that part of the forest before. Certainly the slope of the land was familiar . . . And then the little cavalcade swung around a widespread thicket and he saw where they were going.

The special clearing, its black earth free of all plant life, where the statues stood.

So, he thought dully, the 'place of bare earth' *is* a graveyard. Maybe the statues are grave markers, personalized replicas of the dead. He was about to ask Ilinit, until he remembered in time that not even Rikil had ever spoken to him about the statues. He did not want to offend the Stiks, not then, not when they had allowed him to join their ceremony.

But he thought he would probably learn the truth all too soon, as the Stiks lowered Rikil's stretcher to the ground. They placed her next to a patch of earth in the clearing where the soil seemed to have been loosened, as if cultivated. Ilinit pointed to it, almost proudly.

'Her rejoining place. It has served for many in our kin-group.'

Jonmac frowned. Many Stiks buried in that one small place? It didn't make sense. But still he kept silent, watching as some female Stiks began unwrapping the abundance of cloth from around Rikil. She was lying very still, though her eyes remained open – and she too seemed to look up at the sun now and then, like the other Stiks, as if checking the passage of time. As the cloth was peeled away from her, Jonmac felt an edge of embarrassment. No human had ever seen a Stik unclothed – and Rikil seemed more naked than expected, since most of her golden fur had vanished from her body as well as her head, leaving her skin smooth and unblemished.

But the moment of embarrassment quickly passed. Without clothing or fur, Rikil looked insubstantial, as ethereal as something seen in a dream. And she seemed even more so when, after a gesture from Ilinit, the females carefully lifted her from the stretcher.

'It is time,' Ilinit slowly intoned. 'Her birthing-time was at this moment, this day. Now she is ready to rejoin the ground, which is Source and Renewal of all.'

Tenderly, the females carried Rikil over to the patch of loosened soil, then lowered. And in Jonmac the increased surge of grief was mingled with surprise and curiosity. For they did not place Rikil full-length on the ground.

They lowered her so that only her feet touched the soil. While they held her frail body upright, supporting her.

For several endless moments the group did not move, except that Rikil's head lolled weakly forward and strange tremors swept over her, one after another. Then at last she slowly lifted her head, as if the movement was deeply painful. Her body straightened and stiffened in a series of sharp, quivering jerks. Her eyes, more shadowed than ever, looked at each of the Stiks gathered around her.

Then she moved her gaze to Jonmac, who stood with his face wet with tears. And finally she stared at her group-father, Ilinit. In that moment her mouth opened, contorting as if in a silent scream – her eyes also widened to their fullest extent – her body arched and writhed in a terrible spasm as if shaken by a huge invisible hand.

At last her mouth closed, her eyelids came down. A blankness swept over her face, a stillness over her body.

All the Stiks then drew close around her, for a moment blocking Jonmac's view of her. They were murmuring softly as they enclosed her, soft whispered words that might have been a song or a prayer or merely a farewell. Then they went silent, and all of them stepped back.

Unsupported, Rikil still stood upright, unmoving, not visibly breathing, her face blank and closed, her smooth bare skin gleaming softly in the sunlight.

Jonmac turned away, shaking, unable to bear the sight of his friend standing there, weirdly upright yet lifeless, a corpse turned into a statue. And Ilinit came to join him, looking awed and proud and sad all at once.

'She is rejoined, Onnak,' he said softly. 'Now she is *tistirraka*, earth-dreamer.'

Jonmac swallowed, trying to find his voice. Whether it caused offence or not, he wanted to know. 'What was it, Ilinit, that made her . . . die so young?'

Ilinit turned to him sharply, a strange look in his great eyes. 'What do you mean, Onnak? It was not . . .'

Then he halted, with a blink and a twitch. As if he had been struck by a strange new thought. As if it had just occurred to him that Jonmac the human might not understand every aspect of an event that was perfectly normal and natural to Stiks.

'This is her *time*, Onnak,' Ilinit tried to explain. 'After the right number of turnings of the year, at the same moment on the same day of their birthing, a young Stikesse rejoins the ground. Becomes *tistirraka*. They become unmoving and rooted. Their skin hardens. They look only inward, to the earth-dreaming. And so they remain, nourished by the ground that is Source and Renewal, for another full turning of a year.'

160

'A . . . *year*?' Jonmac repeated faintly, almost unable to breathe.

Ilinit gestured 'yes'. 'When her birthing-day comes again, a year from now, Rikil will lose the roots that now join and anchor her to the ground. She will return to us – as an *adult*, prepared to find a mate and bear her young within the kin-group.'

16

The explanation was like an explosion of white light in Jonmac's mind, leaving him stunned and dizzy. She isn't dead, he yelled silently within himself, repeating the words over and over, hardly able to believe or understand. He peered over at Rikil again, no longer finding it hard to look at her blank and frozen stance. She's *alive* in there, he told himself. Like a coma – or like suspended animation, with life support coming from the *roots* Ilinit said she's grown.

He thought then of the long tendril-like growths on the feet of the 'statue' that the Dusters had placed by the EXTRA base. And sickness struck him as he knew at last why the Stiks had been so horrified when they had found that statue. The uprooting had broken its life-support links to the soil. It hadn't been just a vandalizing of a sculpture. It had been murder.

He gazed around at all the other 'statues' in the clearing. 'Are they all the same?' he asked Ilinit.

'All are earth-dreamers,' the Stik confirmed. 'Some will return soon, other young ones will take their place.'

'Earth-dreamers,' Jonmac echoed, savouring the term. 'Do they really have dreams, when they're like that?'

'So we believe,' Ilinit said. 'I remember when I woke from my own rejoining. I felt that beautiful visions were fleeing in that instant from my mind. I grieved, wanting them back – as all earth-dreamers grieve when they wake. Because they are again severed from the ground, which is Source and Renewal.'

Jonmac sighed, feeling the sadness and sweetness of the belief. 'I wonder what they dream about,' he said, almost to himself.

'No one can say,' Ilinit told him softly. 'But you may find out, Onnak, at your own rejoining.'

Jonmac gestured 'no'. 'Humans . . . don't,' he said. 'We just grow up, slowly, year after year. Our bodies change a bit, in some ways, but that's all.'

Ilinit looked sad. 'Perhaps,' he suggested, 'that is why humans leave their world and journey so tirelessly through the sky to other worlds. Because they have no bonds joining them to their ground.'

'You may be right, Ilinit,' Jonmac murmured. He thought of Rikil, saying much the same thing a while before. And he found himself longing desperately for Rikil to be there, right then, so they could talk about it further.

But it would be a long lonely *year*, he reminded himself, before he would talk with her again. Though having to wait that long was still immeasurably better than what he had believed before, that he would never see her again, alive, at all.

Then a new thought struck him hard. When she did return, she'd be an *adult*, ready to have babies and things. She might not have any time for a human kid who was once her friend . . .

'Ilinit,' he asked carefully, 'when Rikil returns, next year, how quickly will she . . . mate, and everything?'

The Stik made a vague gesture. 'When she finds a suitable male. There are several in other kin-groups who have shown interest.' He peered at Jonmac. 'You understand, Onnak,' he said in a kindly tone, 'that she must take a *Stikessi* mate.'

'Oh, of course,' Jonmac said quickly, feeling his cheeks redden. 'I didn't mean . . . I wasn't thinking of . . .' He gulped, then tried again. 'I just wondered if we'd see much of each other, after . . .'

Ilinit made a short muffled hum that might have been gentle laughter. 'She will still be your friend, Onnak. Taking a mate does not stop friendship. I am sure you will see her often, when she returns. Unless things happen that cannot be foreseen.'

'Like what?' Jonmac asked nervously.

Ilinit laughed again. 'How can I know if they cannot be foreseen? Changes happen, Onnak. It is in the nature of living things to change. Why, more humans might come in a flying thing and carry you away. Who can say?'

Jonmac shook his head, knowing the unlikelihood of that possibility. Then an inner shock rippled through him as he found himself wondering if he would really be ready to *go* if the improbable did happen and a spaceship landed.

Could he just take off after everything that had happened? Could he leave Rikil to come back to life on her next birthday and find him gone without a word?

He was astonished that he could feel that way. It was as if the joy of learning that Rikil would return had drained all the power out of the old horrors, the grief and despair that had haunted him since he was marooned.

But it wasn't just the joy, he realized. It became clear to him that everything he had been doing had been weakening the horrors. All that he had done,

164

and learned, and become. His acceptance of his life on that world, his growing ability to make the most of it and even at times to enjoy it.

Maybe it was natural now, in a way, for him to feel a little reluctant to give up everything he had achieved. And to give up Rikil.

Still, he knew, it wasn't really a problem. There was still almost no chance that a starship would arrive.

But he remained silent and thoughtful as he and Ilinit made their way through the forest back towards the base. Ilinit, too, was companionably silent, as only a Stik could be, until they drew near the base. Then he took his leave, to rejoin his kin-group.

'Do not be too sad during Rikil's absence, Onnak,' he said. 'We in her kin-group will miss her too, but we take joy from her rejoining, and from knowing that she will return.'

'I understand,' Jonmac said. 'But the year will seem a long time, for me, without her.'

'That is so,' Ilinit agreed. 'I know how you have valued her, in your solitude. But you need not be alone, even now, Onnak. All of us in the kin-group are your friends.'

Jonmac blinked, feeling deeply touched. 'Thank you, Ilinit. I would be glad to see you, any of you, any time.' He paused as another thought came to him. 'Would it also be possible for me to . . . to visit Rikil at the place of bare earth?'

'Whenever you wish,' Ilinit said. 'Others will go often, to tend and care for her, but you may certainly go as well.'

So they parted, and Jonmac drifted back to the base. Now, he ordered himself firmly, let's start getting through this year till Rikil's back. Nothing to it. Just keep your head, keep busy and keep on. One day at a time.

It was not, of course, quite as easy as that. Yet also it was not as hard as Jonmac had feared. Life for him went on as before, without too many upheavals, despite the huge gap in every day that had once been filled by Rikil. And then, after a while, Jonmac came up with a brilliant idea that helped him to fill that emptiness and occupy his time.

He thought of it one day when he was again reliving the experience in the clearing, watching Rikil being transformed into a living, rooted statue. Remembering it, picturing each detail, he thought of how his mother and others in the EXTRA team would have been fascinated to see the ceremony and the change. I'll have to remember everything, he thought idly, in case I ever get to tell anyone . . .

That was when he had his brilliant idea. He would write it all down.

The problem was that he had no writing materials. No computers or other data storage equipment, not even a pen or a piece of paper. But – and this was the second part of his brilliant idea – there was the forest.

A particular shortish tree in the forest had a very thick trunk where the bark always seemed to be peeling away in thin layers. Jonmac had often stripped off long sheets of it, just to see how much would come away at one pull.

Thin sheets of soft bark. And if he had a splinter of harder bark, or wood, he could make marks on the soft stuff. He could write on it.

It would be painfully slower than writing on a

keyboard. But that didn't matter. He had, he reminded himself, all the time in the world.

So he gathered the soft bark, in long thin rolls like parchment, and with a sharp piece of harder bark he began. Slowly, patiently, for some hours every day, he wrote and wrote. Beginning with every single detail, as fully as he could, of the morning when Rikil had rejoined the ground.

It was enormously enjoyable, he found, to recreate it all in words, everything that he saw and that was said. It wasn't easy to describe events so that they could be understood, so they came alive, but it could be fun. And it was hugely satisfying when he felt he got some of it just right.

He enjoyed it so much that, when he finished the story of Rikil's ceremony, he went on writing. He began a kind of diary, or journal, setting down everything that had happened since he had been marooned, holding nothing back, not even the worst times when he had been overwhelmed by the horrors. And when he had come up to date, after many days of steady writing, he thought of a new project.

He began to write down as much as he could of the Stik language. He had to invent syllables that seemed to be how Stik words sounded, but they mostly worked well enough. And, he thought with a smile, no other human in the galaxy would be a better judge than he was.

So he gathered more bark, and wrote and wrote. He also continued his diary with accounts of what happened every day from then on. And, when he wasn't writing, it seemed that a good deal *was* happening.

For one thing, he went nearly every day to the sacred clearing to visit Rikil. While there, he talked to her, a kind of one-sided version of all the long rambling conversations they had had. It was nowhere as good as actually talking with her, two-way, but it somehow comforted him, making him feel close to her still.

Usually he talked in his own language, since she couldn't hear. Although sometimes he wondered if perhaps she could in some way, wherever she was. Or maybe, he thought, I'm sometimes part of one of her dreams. And that too was a comforting thought.

Other Stiks often came to the clearing while he was there, to look after their loved ones. They all seemed to know about Jonmac, and showed no surprise at seeing him. And they too murmured softly to the earth-dreamers they were visiting – while tending them, cleaning the hardened, gleaming skin, clearing any sprouting plants from the bare ground.

Almost every day someone from Rikil's kin-group was there to do the same for her. They were always pleased to see Jonmac, and often walked back to the base with him. Otherwise, Ilinit or others of the group would arrive at the base for a visit – and were much amazed at his writing, for the Stiks had no written language. Often, then, they would bring him more sheets of the soft bark, along with other small gifts of food and so on.

So he had some form of regular companionship in Rikil's absence. And he also had the satisfaction of being *accepted*, more and more, by the Stiks. Partly, perhaps, because without really knowing it he was becoming more like them.

For one thing, he was growing rapidly, becoming ever more tall and thin and lanky. He wore the ki-cloth nearly all the time, instead of his own clothes. And he always carried his favourite spear, that Ilinit had given him, whenever he was off the base.

Above all, he was more at home in the forest, more silent and skilful in his movements. He knew it because he was sometimes invited to join Ilinit and the others in a day's hunting and gathering food.

So life went smoothly on for him, more contentedly then he would once have dreamed possible. And the days went on rolling up into weeks, marching on to become months. Until, on a bright chilly day that was nearly halfway towards the day of Rikil's return, Jonmac's peaceful way of life among the Stiks came to a shattering end.

It happened when he was deep in the forest with Ilinit and a younger male from the kin-group, Tisil. They had taken him hunting, intending to visit a distant pool that was rich in a type of leathery, spiny water creature – one of the creatures that the Stiks found tasty and that Jonmac could not imagine eating.

At the pool, Ilinit and Tisil scattered fragments of food on the dark water, then waited motionlessly with spears poised. Jonmac waited in the same way, hardly breathing – and tensed when the water rippled. Something long and sinuous and enormously ugly thrust a wrinkled grey muzzle out of the water, snapping at the bits of food.

Both Stiks struck. Tisil's thrust missed, but Ilinit's spear stabbed into the creature's body. Jerking the spear, Ilinit tried to hoist his prey out on to the ground. But the smooth spear-point pulled loose from the thing's writhing, twisting body. It fell back, and for a fragmentary part of an instant it lay thrashing on the surface of the pool.

Jonmac's spear flashed down, pinning it just below the head, tossing it with a quick flick of his wrist on to the land.

For a moment he stared at it, half-appalled and half-delighted, astonished that he could have moved so quickly and deftly, as if by instinct, when he had never used the spear on anything alive before. And the Stiks began the breathy humming of their laughter.

'You are a good Stikessi hunter, Onnak,' young Tisil said through his laughing. 'You have done better than the group-father himself.'

'It is true,' Ilinit agreed amusedly. 'You become more Stikessi with each day, Onnak. See yourself now. You wear the ki-cloth – you have learned the ways of the forest and how to *be* in the forest – now you show skill with the spear. Who would say you are not a fine young Stikesse?'

They went on laughing, and Jonmac laughed with them. At the same time, he knew how deeply he had been complimented, and pride filled him because of it.

And that was the moment when all laughter stopped.

Because all sound in the forest stopped – drowned by the sudden booming rumble of thunder.

The three hunters looked up, amazed, for the sky was clear, not a storm cloud in sight. But then Jonmac's heart seemed to leap and burst in his chest as he saw it.

He saw a long, glowing trail in the sky, from

where the growing roar of the thunder was erupting.

The glowing trail left by a spaceship, descending.

17

Strange electric jolts fizzed along Jonmac's nerve ends, as his mind began to do dizzying cartwheels that stopped him thinking clearly or even thinking at all. Standing frozen with unbelieving shock, he watched the bright trail of the ship continue on down the sky towards the forest.

In a moment or two the ship would have dropped out of sight behind the trees. But he rushed to a taller tree nearby, swarming up through its branches like a crazed ape. From that height he watched the rest of the ship's descent – down, down, until he saw the flare of the deflector-retros at full impulse, slowing and controlling the landing.

The base, he said to himself numbly. It's landed at the base, or very near it. It could be an EXTRA ship.

When he climbed back to the ground he was trembling slightly, a strange half-smile flickering on his face. And the Stiks watched him, their own expressions unreadable.

'Your kin-group, Onnak?' Ilinit asked. 'They have returned for you?'

Jonmac made a 'maybe' gesture. 'It could be anyone.'

'Could it be ones-of-dust?' young Tisil asked, fingers clenching on the haft of his spear.

'I don't know,' Jonmac said slowly, not having even thought of that possibility. 'It might be.'

'We will go with you to see them, Onnak,' Ilinit

172

told him. 'Then if it is your kin-group, we will be able to say farewell to you before you leave.'

Jonmac stared at him for a moment, his smile fading, while a number of half-formed thoughts swirled and clashed in his mind. Yet he could find words for none of them, and in the end he merely made the 'yes' gesture. 'Let's go, then,' he said.

'But carefully,' Ilinit warned. 'We should learn who they are before they see us.'

The caution was sensible, Jonmac thought, as they set off. Especially when the ship might hold another group of Dusters, ready to start a new reign of ugliness on the planet.

Or they could simply be a different group of traders, strangers from another trading company. Or they could be another sort of space-farers entirely, landing for any number of reasons.

Stop it, he told himself. All I know is that they're humans – they might be friendly – and there's a good chance they can take me home.

But if they plan anything that will harm the Stiks, he thought fiercely, they'll have me to deal with.

And if they go anywhere near the clearing of the *tistirrakai*, and Rikil, I'll kill them.

With that he stopped in his tracks so abruptly that Tisil almost ran into him, with a whistling sound of annoyance. Making the Stik gesture of apology, Jonmac moved on. But as he went, he was thinking with some shock of what he had just said to himself, and what he had been thinking along with that grim threat.

I don't want other humans here, he realized.

His mind was giving him a high-speed, wide-angle review of his life as it then was among the Stiks. How he had it organized, how he contentedly filled his days. How he relished the company of Ilinit and his other Stik friends. How he had taken such pride, that very day, in being told how much he had become like them.

Humans on the planet would spoil it all. They would know nothing of the Stiks or the forest. They would intrude and blunder. And they would want to take *charge*. They would see him as a lost *child* – and would start giving him orders, changing his arrangement of his own life. Ruining everything.

He didn't want them there.

And, as part of the same shocking series of realizations, he knew that he also wasn't ready to *leave*. In a while, perhaps, at a better time . . . But not then. Not when he had just got everything in his life working so well. And certainly not before Rikil returned.

Since Rikil's rejoining, Jonmac had come to feel that if the chance ever came for him to be 'rescued' and leave the planet, it would be easier if that happened after Rikil had found her mate and begun her family. For him, the pain of their parting would be reduced by the excitement of returning home. For Rikil, any pain would be lessened by her involvement in her new life as an adult.

But certainly he did not intend to leave the planet without seeing Rikil again after her return, and properly saying goodbye.

Then he shook his head angrily as if to clear away muzzy thoughts. You're getting ahead of things, he said to himself. You don't know who these people are or whether they're really likely to take you anywhere. See what they're like, and *then* figure things out.

And if they start ordering me around, he thought, or insist on taking me away before I'm ready to go, I'll vanish into the bush with the Stiks. Let them try to find me then . . .

As they drew closer to the EXTRA base, Jonmac and the two Stiks slowed their pace, sliding more stealthily through the brush. Ilinit glanced at Jonmac with what looked like approval as the three of them ghosted through a dense thicket, hardly disturbing a twig. And before long they were able to peer past a veiling mass of branches and see the base.

They had come to it from one side, fairly near to the half-ruined buildings where Jonmac had been living. At the far end of the base, on the great angled support of its undercarriage, loomed the starship of the newcomers.

As he had thought, when he had seen it from a distance, it was the same size and class as the ship of Jonmac's EXTRA team. But its markings, certainly not EXTRA insignia, meant nothing to Jonmac. All he knew was that it was a human ship, and achingly familiar, with the odour of cooling metal from the retros, and the heat-waves crinkling the air above its hull.

Even more achingly familiar was the human appearance of the people he could see moving around what was left of the base.

The people did not wear the tidy grey of the EXTRA uniform, nor the outlandish garb of the Dusters. They wore drab coveralls and jumpsuits, without markings, the normal wear for a starship crew. They seemed perfectly ordinary men and women in every way.

Jonmac had never seen any of them before.

He wasn't sure whether he was glad or sorry that they were strangers. He wasn't sure about any of his feelings, as he crouched in the bush and stared at the first humans he had seen for so long a time. As Ilinit touched his arm, with a look of inquiry in his eyes, Jonmac made a silent gesture that was a Stik hunter's way of saying 'wait and watch'.

Most of the people were clustered, naturally, around the two buildings where Jonmac had lived. They were also talking among themselves in several different conversations, all sounding puzzled and amazed and even a little edgy. And Jonmac found that if he concentrated, he could sort out some of the separate things being said.

'. . . *got* to be humans here,' one voice was saying, 'with all that food and everything . . .'

'. . . the alien weapons and things,' another said. 'Maybe Stiks were living here sometimes . . .'

'. . . Dusters, got to be,' another voice said confidently. 'Only humans likely to be here. Our scanners showed their ship's still here, just where the reports said . . .'

'They got some nerve!' someone said angrily. 'After what they did, to still be *here* . . .'

'They won't be here long,' a different voice interrupted, sounding harsh and eager. 'With the firepower we got, we'll pick 'em up fast or wipe 'em out fast.'

'Blow up their ship and strand them,' someone else said. 'Let EXTRA come pick them up. Less trouble for us.'

As the crowd muttered agreement, Jonmac saw that several of them had flamers slung over their shoulders. He also saw that his Stik friends had noticed the weapons, with some unease.

'These are not ones-of-dust,' Jonmac whispered to them.

The Stiks looked relieved. 'Are they your friends then, Onnak?' Tisil asked.

'I don't know yet,' Jonmac said.

Out on the base, some of the talk had died down as a quieter voice, with authority in it, had begun speaking.

'Wherever the Dusters may be,' the quiet voice said, 'I'd bet a lot that all this isn't their work. When did you ever know Dusters who were *tidy*?'

That caused an outburst of laughter, but with overtones still of puzzlement and wariness. 'You reckon there's *other* humans around?' someone asked.

'I'd say so,' the quieter voice replied. 'Even though the scanners didn't pick up another ship . . .'

The crowd swirled a bit as people turned this way and that, nervously peering at the shadowy forest all around them. Several of them looked directly at the thicket that hid Jonmac and his friends, without seeing anything.

'Quennel could be right,' another calm voice said. 'If it *was* Dusters living here, we'd have found easy-dust.'

'That's so,' someone agreed. 'They don't go very far from their dust.'

'And why would they be here,' someone else put in, 'when their ship is so far from here?'

As the crowd murmured and swirled in more unsettled movement, Jonmac heard a startled voice call out from within one of the two buildings. 'Just look at all *this*!'

And Jonmac's heart sank as the speaker emerged

– a small dark woman clutching an armful of rolls of thin bark. Jonmac's writings.

'This is *strange!*' the woman said. She took the rolls to the quiet-spoken man who had been named as Quennel – a tall red-haired man who seemed to be in command.

'Very strange,' the man agreed, taking a roll of bark and opening it. 'Look at this – a lot of letters all jumbled up, with words written beside them. Sort of like . . .'

'Like a dictionary!' the woman said.

'Right.' Quennel glanced around, frowning. 'Have those other two come out of the ship yet? They should see this. They might know what it's about.'

'They'll be along,' said a short man next to him. 'The woman, she was kind of upset, crying, hanging back. Not sure what she might run into out here . . .'

Quennel nodded. 'Maybe you could go and get them. Tell them we didn't find any . . . remains, or anything upsetting like that. And tell her about this writing. She's the one who might figure it out.'

As he spoke, unthinkingly, he slightly crumpled the roll of bark in his hand. And others were grabbing for other rolls, opening them curiously and carelessly. Which was the last straw for Jonmac.

He didn't know who they were or what they wanted. Despite their weapons, he felt a little reassured by their apparent dislike of Dusters. But most of all, right then, he felt deeply annoyed at their rough handling of his personal things.

And in part of himself he also enjoyed the high drama of the moment – as, wrapped in ki-cloth and spear in hand, he stepped silently out of the forest, into view.

'Be careful with those things!' he called out sharply. 'They're *mine!*'

Every person in the area whirled towards him – and then froze as if solidified, in often quite comic positions of astonishment and shock and fright. In that moment of paralyzed stillness, Jonmac moved forward, scowling at those still clutching his rolls of bark.

Then he halted, as a movement at the starship caught his eye.

Two people had appeared in the opening of the ship's airlock. A rangy man with greying hair, and a slim pretty woman who looked as if she had been weeping.

Su Lowde and Coln Robett. Standing frozen, staring at Jonmac with shocked, disbelieving eyes.

18

'You could almost say the Dusters saved your life,' Coln Robett told Jonmac. 'The Stiks might have killed you in that attack if they'd found you first.'

They were sitting on the ground, with Su, between the two buildings. Su, wearing a wide shaky smile, sat as close to Jonmac as she could get – gazing at him and often touching him as if to be sure he was really there – while Robett had been explaining how and why they had returned.

Apparently Quennel and the others were a survey crew, on their way to a different world, an uninhabited planet in a nearby star system. Since they were passing quite close, in space-travel terms, Robett and Su had travelled with them, paying a large sum to divert the starship to land briefly on the world of the Stiks.

After the EXTRA team had fled, Su had been nearly crazed with grief, certain that Jonmac had died during the attack on the base. On Earth, she had been unable to bear the thought of her dead son lying on an indifferent alien world. So she and Robett had returned to find Jonmac's remains and return them to Earth for a proper burial.

And now, sitting next to her very alive son, she listened wide-eyed to his account of how he had survived the attack on the base, before he had been marooned.

'I suppose the Stiks might have got me,

Jonmac replied to Robett. He was finding it hard to imagine Stiks being dangerous to him, though he clearly recalled the attack, and Loysel writhing in his blood from a spear-wound. 'Like they got Loysel,' he added uneasily. 'Did . . . did he die?'

'No, he's all right,' Robett said, 'and no one else got hurt.' He seemed to be half-smiling. 'Loysel just got a nasty flesh wound. Had a hard time sitting down for some weeks.'

There was a general ripple of laughter. The other people from the ship had hung back at first, out of respect for the emotional reunion between mother and son. But they had been creeping closer, listening enthralled to Jonmac's story.

'And you'll be glad to know,' Robett added, 'that EXTRA has pushed the authorities into a major interplanetary clean-up against the Dusters. To put them out of business for good, wherever they are.'

'From what you say, Jonnie,' Su put in, 'it sounds like the Stiks did their *own* clean-up, here.'

Jonmac nodded. 'They were turning against the Dusters anyway, I think. But when the Dusters went for the *tistirrakai* . . .'

'The what?' Su asked, startled.

Jonmac realized he had used the Stik word. 'What we thought were statues,' he said. 'But they're . . . It's kind of a long story.'

Everyone seemed perfectly willing for him to tell it, right then. Until someone at the edge of the group gave a muffled shriek, others gasped, and there was a general flurry of movement and weapons.

At the edge of the base stood two motionless Stiks. Ilinit and Tisil, who – Jonmac remembered guiltily – had been waiting patiently all that time.

'Don't shoot!' he said sharply. 'They're looking for me!'

Then he went quickly to the Stiks, making the gesture for apology. 'Ilinit, I'm sorry,' he said in their language.

Ilinit's gesture set the apology aside. 'It is no matter, Onnak. We come only to know that all is well, and that these are friends.'

'Better even than that,' Jonmac said. 'Among them are two from my kin-group who were here before. My own birth-mother, and our . . . our group-father.'

Ilinit's eyes brightened. 'That is a gladness, Onnak. We share your joy.' Then the brightness faded. 'You will leave now? They will take you away into the sky?'

'I don't know,' Jonmac said hesitantly. 'I'm not sure . . . if I want to go just yet.'

'But if your kin-group wish it,' Tisil said, 'you surely *must* go. It is what must be.'

'Perhaps,' Jonmac said. 'But I wanted to speak to Rikil before I left.'

Ilinit touched his arm understandingly. 'Talk of it with those of your kin-group. Decide with them, together. *That* is what must be.' He glanced at the great ship looming beyond them. 'And if you decide to go, Onnak, come to seek us to say farewell.'

He and Tisil made the friendship gesture, which Jonmac returned, and then the two Stiks melted into the forest. And Jonmac found all the humans staring at him, open-mouthed, in awe.

'Jonnie,' Su breathed. 'I wouldn't have believed anyone could get so fluent in that language . . .'

'Sounded just like a Stik yourself,' Robett agreed, grinning. 'Look a lot like one too.'

Jonmac shrugged. 'The Stiks have been my friends. They've given me a lot and taught me a lot. Especially Rikil.'

'Yes, the little female,' Su said, remembering. 'Where is she now?'

'She's . . .' Jonmac took a deep breath. 'That's part of the long story I mentioned, about what we thought were statues. I wrote it all down there.' He pointed to the rolls of bark that had been placed nearby. 'You could look at it later if you want. But basically, what happens is . . .'

And he gave them a quick summary of a young Stik's transformation into an 'earth-dreamer' and then to adulthood.

For a quiet moment after he was done, all the people sat in silence. 'It's very beautiful,' Su said at last. 'And to think that you were allowed to see it . . . As if you were one of them . . .'

Robett smiled. 'EXTRA will wish they could go on trading here, now that you're so close to the Stiks.'

'Why can't they?' Jonmac asked.

'You know the rule,' Robett said. 'EXTRA automatically lost its licence for this planet when we abandoned the base . . .'

Suddenly he slapped his forehead, looking astonished. 'Of course! The base *wasn't* abandoned, Jonmac – because *you* were here! An EXTRA employee! So the licence shouldn't have been revoked!'

'And we can all vouch for that,' Quennel said

183

in his quiet voice from where he was sitting and listening with the others.

'Looks like you should've been *trading*, lad, all this while,' said another man, grinning.

'I didn't have to trade,' Jonmac said flatly. 'The Stiks *gave* me things. Ki-cloth, weapons, carvings, food . . . And the cargo holds of the Duster ship are *full* of cloth.'

That caused a buzz of excited talk. 'I'd say all that belongs to you, Jonmac,' Robett said at last. 'By the laws of salvage, because you were the last survivor. Isn't that so, Captain Quennel?'

'It surely is,' Quennel said, eyes twinkling.

Robett grinned. 'So you can sell the ki-cloth to EXTRA which will make them happy. And with the Stik artefacts as well, you could be considerably rich.'

Su laughed at Jonmac's amazed expression. 'EXTRA will be *very* happy with you, Jonnie. Now they can go on trading here – and all this data that you've written down will make things easy for the next trading team.'

Robett nodded. 'You can write your own future, Jonmac. EXTRA will surely give you full trader status with a nice fat contract. And a good long expenses-paid leave on Earth, after all your time here . . .'

'Wait, wait!' Jonmac cried. It was all too much, too huge and unexpected a prospect rushing at him. 'I have friends here. Not just aliens. I owe them . . . everything. I can't just fly off to Earth and let a lot of strangers move in on them.'

'But, Jonnie . . .' Su began.

He raised a hand to stop her. 'I mean this, Su. I can't turn my back on my friends. Most of all, I want to be here when Rikil returns. After that, maybe things will be different. But I have to be here.' He stared around at them all, willing them to understand. 'This is something I've thought about a lot,' he went on. 'About getting to be friends with aliens on other worlds. Getting close to them, learning their ways, understanding their lives. Not just trading a lot of junk for whatever we want from them. There has to be more to it than that.'

Su looked at him with a mixture of pride and sadness. 'You've grown up, haven't you, Jonnie? Not just taller and a bit older. Grown up.'

'Young people do that,' Robett said calmly. 'And Jonmac has found his own words for something that a lot of people on Earth have been thinking, about our dealings with aliens.' He studied Jonmac with approval. 'You're the first to put those ideas into practice, Jonmac. To show that it *can* be done, on another world. EXTRA is going to be very interested. And it's going to need you, and people like you, to go on doing it, on other worlds.'

Jonmac nodded slowly, feeling a little dazzled. 'That's *it*, Coln. That's what I'd like to do. Not just be a trader. Be a . . . a . . .'

'An ambassador,' Su said softly.

He nodded again, thinking about it, about all the possibilities for the years ahead. Then abruptly he shook his head, while unconsciously making the sharp Stik gesture that meant 'stop'.

'But I still don't want to leave here,' he said, 'until Rikil's back. And until I'm sure any new team will do things right.'

'Jonnie,' his mother began. 'You said Rikil won't be out of the clearing for *months*. We can't stay here that long . . .'

'*I* can,' Jonmac said bluntly.

Su frowned. 'That's ridiculous! You want to go *on* being marooned here, all alone, even after we've found you?'

'I'm not alone here,' Jonmac pointed out, stubbornness glinting in his eyes. 'The Stiks are my friends. And I won't be marooned any more, now you know I'm here, and with a new team coming from EXTRA. And . . . I'm just not *ready* to leave yet.' He glanced at Robett as if in appeal. 'Anyway, there's plenty more to be learned about this world. I won't be wasting my time.'

As Su was about to speak again, Robett put his hand on her arm. He had been watching Jonmac closely, and had begun slowly nodding.

'We're forgetting one point,' Robett said. 'If we all leave, and take Jonmac with us, the base *will* then be abandoned. Which would revoke EXTRA's trading licence.'

Su shook her head, desperately searching for some argument, some way to avoid being parted from her son again. But again Robett stopped her.

'You said he's grown up, Su,' Robett went on quietly. 'Let him *be* grown up. It's hard, but it's necessary. Someone from EXTRA has to stay, and Jonmac's the best-equipped as well as the one who wants to. Let him decide, as a grown-up should – with your blessing.'

Su opened her mouth, then closed it again. Wordlessly she looked at her son, her eyes filming with tears as she slowly, reluctantly, nodded.

'Will you two come on with us, then?' Captain Quennel asked Robett.

'Thanks, but no,' Robett said. 'I'm thinking

about taking that Duster ship back to Earth, with Su. We have to tell EXTRA the news – and sell the ki-cloth and the ship to make Jonmac rich.' He grinned. 'Then we'll make sure we're part of any new trading team EXTRA sends back here.'

Quennel nodded. 'That team will have a better start than any other traders ever, with what the lad can teach them about this place.'

'Right,' Robett agreed, still grinning. 'Which is why Su and I will also make sure EXTRA gives Jonmac full trader status – and a bonus.'

'Make him even richer,' Quennel said with a laugh.

Jonmac looked from one to the other, smiling widely as his future unfolded before him. Including his continuing stay on the world of the Stiks, waiting for Rikil. And then, in a while, when the time was right, travels to other worlds – to make other alien friends, to face other challenges. It was a breathtaking prospect, without any flaws or shadows that he could see.

Until Su introduced one.

She had fought back tears, fought to accept what every parent must someday accept, that children will always grow up into separate lives of their own. So the smile she gave Jonmac was brave, and loving, and accepting – with also a tinge of laughter.

'What we'll do,' she told him, 'is leave you a power source, with a computer and software. So you can catch up on some schoolwork, while you're here.'

Everyone laughed at the sudden dismay on Jonmac's face. Then they all got up and trooped away to look at the Duster ship, and to take the first steps towards Jonmac's, and everyone's, incredible future.

THE END

NOTE TO THE READER

In the summer of 1815 one of the first settlements in western Canada almost came to a premature end. It had been set up by an established, royally chartered fur-trading group called the Hudson's Bay Company and, by 1815, it was thriving (on the Red River in what is now Manitoba). But that year it was attacked and mostly destroyed by wild western Indians, who had been incited by some unruly and unlicensed fur traders known as Northwesters.

Some of the essential elements of that brief, violent episode have been borrowed, and very freely adapted, for the background and plot of this story.

ABOUT THE AUTHOR

Douglas Hill was born in Manitoba, in western Canada, and grew up in Saskatchewan. After graduating with a B.A. (Hons) in English, he moved to London in 1959 and began to earn a living as a writer. He began by working in journalism and by writing non-fiction books on a range of subjects, but turned to writing science fiction and fantasy for young readers in the late 1970s. The author of more than twenty titles for young readers, including the well-known *Last Legionary* quintet and the *Colsec* trilogy, *World of the Stiks* is his first title to be published by Bantam Books.

He lives in north London and has one grown-up son.

HELL ON EARTH

ANTHONY MASTERS

Crash-landed in the rain forest!

Alone in the Amazonian rain forest, their plane in flames and the pilot dead, eighteen-year-old Joe and his friend Sam face an almost hopeless situation. Hundreds of kilometres away from anywhere, equipped only with a knife, a compass and a map scrawled by a desperate, dying man, they are to need every ounce of their courage and strength to survive within the great, remote silence of the forest.

And Joe and Sam must face more than the natural dangers of this alien, primitive world. For they have a valuable stone belonging to an Indian tribe – a stone that could save the forest from the ravages of the timber companies. But there are others after the stone – evil, merciless men who are prepared to kill anyone who gets in their way. . .

A gripping adventure, packed with action and authentic detail.

0 553 405225